# DIRT BIKE
# RACER

THE **#1**
**SPORTS SERIES**
**FOR KIDS**

# DIRT BIKE
# RACER

LITTLE, BROWN AND COMPANY
Books for Young Readers
New York   Boston

To Ted and Pearl

Little, Brown and Company

Hachette Book Group USA
237 Park Avenue, New York, NY 10017
Visit our Web site at www.lb-kids.com

www.mattchristopher.com

First Paperback Edition: September 1986

The characters and events in this book are fictitious. Any similarity to real persons, living or dead, is coincidental and not intended by the author.

Matt Christopher® is a registered trademark of
Matt Christopher Royalties, Inc.

Library of Congress Cataloging-in-Publication Data

Christopher, Matthew F.
    Dirt bike racer / Matt Christopher.
    ISBN 978-0-316-14053-9
    Summary: Twelve-year-old Ron Baker finds a mini bike while scuba diving
and, with the help of a former motorcycle rider and racer, restores the bike
and enters competitions.
    [1. Minibikes — Fiction.    2. Motorcycle racing— Fiction.]    I. Title.
    PZ7.C458DK   813.54 [Fic]
                                                        79-745

30  29  28  27

COM-MO

Printed in the United States of America

# 1

Ordell, NY — The severe windstorm that lashed at this bayside city last night also took its toll of a houseboat that had been moored at Tecumseh Harbor.

Torn from its moorings, the houseboat was blown down Pumpkin Head Lake where high waves thrashed it about mercilessly. According to its owners, Mr. and Mrs. Stuart Kline of River Park, much of the equipment on the houseboat was lost in the lake, including a new set of dishes, a stove, a color television set, and a dirt bike . . .

Tony talked me into it. And it wasn't easy. You would think that because my father was a former scuba-diving pro (he taught it), I would follow gladly in his footsteps. Right? Not so. I only went into the sport because of my father. For some reason water doesn't appeal to me that much.

Anyway, after about fifteen minutes on the phone, Tony and I hung up. I turned to glance at the clock in the kitchen and caught my mother looking at it, too. She had the pantry door open, taking inventory of the depleting stock, and making a list of it on a pad.

"Well," she said, in that half-serious, half-amused way of hers. "Seventeen minutes of a very scintillating conversation. Broke the record by about five to eight minutes. What was that all about, anyway?"

"Tony wants me to go scuba diving with him," I said.

"Where?"

"Pumpkin Head Lake."

Pumpkin Head Lake is about three-quarters of a mile south of our home, and an ideal lake for scuba diving. It's small — only six miles long, a half mile wide at its broadest point, and a hundred and fifteen feet deep at its lowest point. We never scuba dived at anywhere near that depth, of course, but I like to mention it because my father has. Not once, but several times. He's really a skilled diver, that guy.

"Where on Pumpkin Head Lake?" my mother asked.

"Off Turkey Point," I said.

That's about two miles from the north end of the lake. Pumpkin Head, running from northeast to southwest, looks like a blue slash mark on a map. It's been stocked with trout and bass, and sometimes my father and I — or Tony and I — take out our fishpoles and bring home a mess of them.

"How deep is it there? And is anybody else going besides you and Tony?"

"Oh, Ma, you know I never dive more than twenty-five or thirty feet," I told her. "And it's less than that there. And, no, nobody else is going. Now, can I get a move on? I told Tony I'd be there in fifteen minutes."

She smiled. Whenever I see my mother smile I always think that she has such white teeth she'd be a knockout on one of those TV commercials. "Okay, scuba man. Move on," she said.

"Thank you," I said, and bowed out of the room.

I got my gear, piled it into the rear pannier of my bike, and pedaled off to Tony's house. Tony — whose full name is Tony Franco — lives on Pine Street. I've known him all my life, which is going on to thirteen years. But it's only been the last couple of years that we have become pals. Don't ask me why. It just happened.

I didn't see him around when I got there.

"Are you looking for Tony, Ron?" Mrs. Franco called from the kitchen door.

"Yeah," I said. "He said he'd be waiting for me."

"Here I am!" I heard a voice yell. Tony's voice seemed about an octave higher than an owl's. I'd recognize it anywhere.

I looked around. "Where?" I asked.

"Here!" he said. "Underneath the porch! Wait a sec! I'll be right out!"

His mother chuckled. "Nervana chased a mouse or something under there, and can't find her way out. So Tony had to crawl in after her."

Nervana is their cat. A calico feline with six toes on each paw. As for me, I wouldn't give a dime for any cat. One scratched me once, just because I wanted to pet it. Since then, the wider the gap between a cat and me, the better.

A few seconds later Tony crawled out from under the porch, Nervana clutched under his right arm. The instant he let her loose she meowed and bounded off.

4

He got up and brushed himself off. "Dumb cat," he said. "That's the third time she got trapped under there. Too dumb to know how to find her way out."

"Can't you plug up the hole where she goes in?" I asked.

He looked at me. "Ever hear of procrastination? That means never do today what you can do tomorrow. It's my dad's favorite motto."

I shrugged. "Don't knock it. It has its good points." I looked around for his diving gear. "You ready to go?"

"In a minute," he said.

He trotted up on the porch and came back down with the gear. Then he got his bike out of the garage, placed the gear into its rear pannier, and we rode off.

"Be home before five, now!" his mother called after him.

"I will!" he called back to her.

We rode through the streets, crossed the bridge on Englewood, then took the shortcut through the park. With the Fourth of July just behind us, this was a nice time of year. The trees were flush with green leaves, the grass was like an emerald sea, and the few flowers in bloom were like frosting on a cake.

I heard a hum behind us that quickly grew into a roar. A couple of seconds later two motorcyclists sped by us, one on our left, the other on our right. They both goosed their engines as they went by, then fired their plugs to make them sound like pistol shots. This was against the city of Ordell's law. But, with no cops around, a minor thing like firing spark plugs wasn't going to stop Lug Maneer and Skitch Bentley from having their fun.

"Punks," said Tony. "I wonder whose motorcycle they stripped last night."

"I'm glad we've got bikes," I said. "There's nothing on these things they could use."

"Don't bet on it," said Tony.

Twice during the last two years Lug and Skitch had been arrested for stealing parts off someone's motorcycle. The last arrest was about eight or nine months ago. Since then there had been no complaints about stripped bikes. But how long that would last was anybody's guess.

In a little while the two came buzzing back, again passing by with us in the middle. Tony and I waved at them. They didn't wave back.

"Big shots," mumbled Tony.

Tony and I rode as far as we could out on Turkey Point, which was a strip of land extending out into the lake. A tree grew on the end of it, looking so lonely you wondered how it could survive.

There were also some bushes, which we used to hide in as we stripped and put on our trunks and scuba outfits. Tony and I used the single air-cylinder tanks, which were plenty for the kind of diving we did. We pulled on our flippers, checked our pressure and depth gauges, then adjusted our face masks with the breathing tubes attached to them. All set, we waded out into the water till it was up to our waists. Then we dove in.

We swam out about a hundred yards. Tony and I checked back on each other — the old buddy bit — every couple of minutes to see that the other one was all right.

We frightened individual fish — some over two feet long — and a school of sunfish so numerous you wouldn't believe. All at once I got the scare of my life. I looked up and could see Tony's fast-moving flippers, but nothing else! And then even the flippers had disappeared!

"Tony! You jerk!" I wanted to yell.

What he had done, of course, was swim down over a ledge. I flippered hard toward the spot and saw him diving deeper into the water. The position of the sun made it easy to see the underwater contours. And what I saw was a skin diver's dreamworld. The ledge went straight down, like a wall. Weeds grew along the sides, their long slender leaves waving back and forth as if they were keeping time to music.

But the drop was too deep for Tony and me. It could go down to forty or fifty feet. Maybe more. Neither one of us had ever dived more than thirty feet before. I was sure we could. But we had made a promise to our parents. Thirty feet was the limit until we got a couple of years older. Then we could dive deeper. Until then . . .

Two bright shining objects suddenly flashed below me. I looked for Tony and saw him swimming toward the left. Whether he had seen the shining objects I didn't know. Tony's not half as curious as I am. If he saw something strange he might want to check it out, or he might not. It always depended on how he felt at the moment.

Me, I'm like that curious cat. Those two shining objects might not have been anything but bottles. But there was something about them that deserved a closer look. At least in my opinion they did.

But I didn't want to swim to them alone. I didn't want to get too wide a gap between Tony and me. You never know when something could happen — to the breathing apparatus, to the pressure gauge, to anything — and you'd want your partner nearby to give you help.

I was about to cuss Tony for ignoring that unwritten law when I saw him look back. Quickly I motioned him to come forward.

He trod water awhile, staring at me, and I motioned to him again. More insistently this time. Then I pointed down toward the shining objects.

I saw him check his depth gauge, and I checked mine. Twenty-two feet. And we had been swimming about five minutes. We had from eight to ten minutes of diving time left before we had to surface.

I started to motion to him again, but he was already swimming toward me. I turned and headed down toward the two shining objects. I figured they must be about fifteen to twenty feet deeper.

*I'm sorry, Mom and Dad! But I've just got to see what those things are down there!*

Gradually I began to distinguish the outlines of — what do you know — a bike. Not the ordinary, pedal-type two-wheeler.

But a dirt bike.

# 2

It lay on its side near a giant boulder. The two shining objects turned out to be its handlebars. The rest of its small compact body was turning green from algae.

I couldn't get over it. A dirt bike! How did it get here? How long had it been here? And what in the world were we going to do about it?

I looked around at Tony, the question in my eyes: *Well? Are we just going to sit here and look at it? Or shall we do something about it?*

Minibike and motocross races have become pretty popular in our neighborhood. Mike, Tony's sixteen-year-old brother, has a Honda. He's had a bike since he was eleven years old, starting with a small Suzuki, and getting the Honda only last year.

I've envied him and other motorbike owners for a long time. I had even dreamed of owning one of these babies myself someday. But it had been just a dream.

I swam around the bike, noticing that part of its wheels were sunk in the sand. I grabbed its handles and pulled. The bike moved easily, stirring up the sand. And I stared at Tony.

*No,* his eyes said as he shook his head. And *no,* again.

I frowned at him, and shook my head vigorously. *Darn it, Tony!* I wanted to shout. *I found this bike! I want to get it out of here!*

*No!* his head shook again.

The jerk! I thought. Wait till you want something from me!

I didn't give up. If he wasn't going to help me, I'd get the bike out by myself. And if I weren't able to do it alone, I'd get my father to help me.

Turning away from Tony, I grabbed the handlebars of the bike and started to lift it. But, even though being in the water made it lighter, it was still too heavy for me to lift.

I cursed silently, and was about to give up, when Tony grabbed the rear fender — reluctantly, judging by the shake of his head — and we began to swim up with it.

We raised it to the surface and swam with it to the tip of Turkey Point. It was heavier now, but we managed to pull it to shore, where I was glad to take off my mask, the air cylinder, and the fins. Tony did the same. Then we both looked at our underwater treasure.

"I wonder how it got in there?" I said. "Nobody in his right mind would toss a beauty like that into a lake."

Tony didn't answer immediately, and I saw his forehead crease, as if he were trying to remember something.

"Don't tell me you know something about this?" I said.

"I think I do," he answered. "Remember back about two years ago when a houseboat was damaged in a storm, and one of the things lost from it was a dirt bike?"

"Hey, that's right," I said. "I remember." The whole picture wasn't too clear yet, but I vaguely remembered about the storm and a damaged houseboat.

"Well, none of the things were ever found. This must be the minibike that was lost."

I don't know why I happened to turn just then. Maybe it was intuition. But I had a feeling that we were being watched.

Sure enough, we were. I got a slight shock, because the two guys who were sitting on their motorcycles about a hundred feet away from us, staring at us, usually came on strong. They had probably arrived just before Tony and I had surfaced with the minibike.

"Look who's watching us like vultures," I said.

"Yeah, Lug Maneer and Skitch Bentley," observed Tony. "The two most honest guys in Ordell."

They were wearing dark sunglasses. Lug was sitting with his arms crossed over his chest, chewing gum. Skitch was leaning forward, his elbows on the handlebars of his motorcycle.

I didn't like their presence one bit.

"I don't trust them," I said to Tony.

"Ignore them," he said. "And let's start washing this baby off before the green stuff dries on it."

"Wash it? With what?"

"Water. What else? When you get it home you can use a brush, and rags."

14

I stared at him. "Look, you helped me bring it up. It's as much yours as it is mine."

"Don't be ridiculous," he said. "You're the one who found it."

My heart started pumping hard. "Tony, are you sure that you —"

"Look, let's get it washed so that when you have it home your father won't want to throw it into the junk pile," Tony interrupted. He stepped closer to it and rubbed off the slimy algae that partially covered a name.

"'Jonny Jo,'" he read. "You know something, Ron? I think you've found yourself a real sharp little racer here. I read Mike's bike magazines once in a while, and I remember reading an article or two about the Jonny Jo. Yes, sirree, baby. I think you've found yourself something. Unless the Klines try to take it back from you."

"The Klines? They're the people who had owned the houseboat?"

"That's right."

"I'll have to check on that," I said.

I wished he hadn't mentioned the Klines. All the time we were washing the slime off the mini, the

15

possibility of their reclaiming the bike was the only thing I could think about.

I heard the roar of engines, and turned to see Lug and Skitch leave. I sighed with relief. Good riddance, I thought. Maybe they were living a straight life lately, but if any two guys looked as if they were ready to break the golden rule any minute, it was those two.

Getting the bike home was our next problem. My father was working, and he had the car. I wracked my brain and finally thought of Mr. Reston, our next-door neighbor. Not only did he work nights, but he had a utility trailer. The mini would fit into it easily.

I mentioned my idea to Tony, and he agreed with it.

We used our locker room in the bushes again, dried ourselves with the towels, and got into our clothes.

Then, while Tony remained to watch over the mini — which looked a lot different now after the wash — I biked to Mr. Reston's house and found him putting in a new kitchen sink. It seemed that the Restons were always putting in something new, or buying new furniture. My mother said that they always bought inexpensive stuff, which seldom lasted long. A good reason, I suppose, for buying new things fairly regularly.

I gave Mr. Reston the whole story, and got the answer I was afraid I would.

"Can't till I get this doggone sink in, Ronnie," he said. "Can you wait for another half hour or so? Be glad to bring your bike home then. What kind of a bike did you say it was?"

"A dirt bike, what they call a minibike," I said.

"It's got a motor?"

"Oh, yes. A single-cylinder, two-cycle engine," I explained. "It should fit into your trailer easily, Mr. Reston."

"Oh, I'm sure it will. But it'll still be half an hour." He looked at his wristwatch. "It's a quarter of four now. I'll see you about a quarter after, Ron."

"Okay. I'll wait for you at Turkey Point, Mr. Reston. Tony's there, watching over the bike."

"Fine."

I rode back and told Tony the story. There was nothing to do but sit on the sand and wait.

# 3

**W**e talked, our conversation covering Lug Maneer and Skitch Bentley, and the Klines, who, Tony was more and more convinced, had owned the Jonny Jo. I was beginning to wonder if fixing up the minibike to get it running again would be worth it, if they eventually would come around and claim it.

It wasn't till four-thirty that Mr. Reston arrived, pulling the trailer behind his car.

"Sorry, boys," he said apologetically. "Took me longer to finish the job than I expected." He saw the algae-stained minibike, and his eyes widened. "Wow! So that's it, is it? Think you can ever get it to run again?"

"I hope so," I said.

"Well, let's get it on the trailer."

It was no job lifting it on. There was also plenty of room for our bikes and scuba equipment.

Mr. Reston drove off. At home again he backed up into our driveway, and we lifted off the three bikes.

"Thanks a million, Mr. Reston," I said. "Can I pay you something? At least to cover the gas?"

"Don't insult me, Ron," he said. "I'm willing to give you and your parents a hand anytime. You know that."

"Thanks, Mr. Reston," I said, smiling. "I'm sure glad we have you for a neighbor."

My mother came out on the side porch, wondering what the commotion was all about. Then she stood there with her mouth open as she stared at the minibike.

"Where in blazes did that animal come from?" she asked finally.

I told her. All the while she kept staring at me as if I had lost my mind. Nobody's eyes can get bigger than my mother's when she sees something that catches her by surprise. And, of course, the minibike did.

19

"What do you think you're going to do with it when it's all cleaned and fixed up?" she asked wonderingly.

"Ride it. Naturally," I said. "What does a guy do with a bike?"

"Watch your tongue, young man," she snapped, shifting her eyes from the bike to me. "Or I'll have you take that thing back to where you got it from."

"I'm sorry, Ma," I said. "I didn't mean it to sound like that."

I didn't think she'd ever force me to do that, but I wasn't going to take any chances.

Tony and I scrubbed the bike with a couple of brushes, then kept wiping it with paper towels. YZ80C showed up on its side.

"YZ eighty C," I read. "Is that the model, Tony?"

"Right."

I wondered what my father would say when he got home from work and saw it. He never told me whether he had ever owned a motorcycle. We had talked about a lot of things he did when he was young — his fishing, his interest in skin diving. But never about motorcycling.

Would he care if I kept it? Some fathers wouldn't let their kids own a motorbike even if it were given to them. The strongest reason they had against it was the danger of getting into an accident. But there was that danger with a bicycle, too. Or with a tricycle, a skateboard, or even a sled, for that matter.

Tony and I were still at it when my father's blue sedan pulled up into the driveway. He slowed down alongside us, stared at the bike, then at me.

"Well," he said, "whose is it?"

I wet my lips, which, for some reason, had suddenly become dry. "Mine," I answered.

He stared at me. "Yours? Where did you get it?"

"We pulled it out of Pumpkin Head Lake. Tony and I were scuba diving there this afternoon, and we saw it in water about — well, I don't know — maybe fifty feet deep."

He stared hard at me. "Didn't you have your depth gauge with you?"

"Yes."

"Then you should've known how deep it was."

My heart pounded. Why did he have to bring up my breaking the rule now?

"I should have," I said, my insides hurting. "But I can't remember the depth exactly, Dad. I saw this dirt bike down there, and I didn't think much more

21

about how deep I was going. I just know it couldn't have been more than fifty feet, because I had checked my depth gauge just before that and it read forty feet."

He seemed to accept that as final, then drove the car into the garage. I sighed with relief and looked at Tony.

"I don't know," I said uncomfortably. "Maybe *you* should have it, Tony."

"Not on your life," he said. "She's your baby."

I wondered then if I had picked up a monster instead of just a dirt bike.

After a while Tony had to leave; it was getting near suppertime.

"Want me to ask Mike to come and look it over for you?" he offered. "He can tell you exactly what parts you'll need fixed or changed to get that bike running again."

"I sure would appreciate it," I said. "But whether I can ever afford the parts for it is another thing."

Tony glanced at my father, then back at me. "See you later," he said.

He put his scuba equipment and towel into the pannier of his bike and pedaled off.

"I won't mind your having that bike," said my father, who was showing more interest in it now than I'd expected. "But there are a couple of things you had better check on first."

I looked at him. "Like what?"

"Like who owned it before. I can call up Dick Thomas, my attorney, and see what the law is regarding that. The second thing is, you'll have to find your own way to pay for the parts."

Some of the weight disappeared from my chest. "Why, sure, Dad." I smiled, thrilled that he'd let me keep the bike. "I'll look for a job. I'm not a little kid anymore."

"Right. And once you get it running — because with Mike Franco's help I'm sure you will — you'll have to learn to give it more respect than you would an ordinary bicycle. This thing has a single-cylinder, two-cycle engine. And it eats up miles much quicker than a bike."

"I know that, Dad. You don't have to tell me," I said.

Our eyes met. "I'm sure you do," he replied, smiling. "I just wanted to remind you of it. I don't want you to get hurt."

"I'll remember that," I promised.

Safe driving, safe diving, safety in anything came first in my father's book. It had been impressed on him when he had taken up skin and scuba diving. And he had impressed it on me when he had taught me how to dive.

The porch door opened and my mother stuck her head out. "You men ready to leave that toy for a few minutes?" she asked. "Dinner's ready."

We grinned. "We'll be right in, Dorothy," said my father.

We went in, washed our hands, and sat down to eat. Our topic while eating dinner was the topic of the moment, the minibike. Would I have to have a license? Could I drive it on the streets? Did I intend to race it?

My answers to those questions were, "I don't know yet. I just found the bike. Give me time."

I finished eating before my mother and father and fidgeted in my chair.

"Pretty excited about that bike, aren't you?" said my father.

I shrugged. "Yes. I guess I am."

Well, of course I was. I hadn't said that I planned on racing it. But, in the back of my mind, that's what

I was thinking I would like to do. I couldn't wait till I had all the new parts for it. Till it was fixed up and ready to go. I don't think I was ever more excited about anything in my life than getting that minibike to go again.

But first my father had to make an important call to his lawyer. There was no sense in my doing anything until after that call was made.

He telephoned his lawyer that evening. When he hung up he had a sad look on his face. My chin must have dropped a foot.

Then suddenly his eyes flashed, and the sad look changed into a smile.

"It's okay!" I cried. "I can keep the bike!"

He nodded. "Dick remembered that situation. The Klines had everything insured, and were paid by the insurance company, making it free and clear for you to keep the bike."

"Hey, that's just great! Just *great!*"

Tony and Mike came over at seven o'clock. Mike was about half a head taller than Tony and twenty pounds heavier. Three nights a week he worked at the movie theater, taking tickets from the customers.

"Hey, a YZ eighty C Jonny Jo," he exclaimed enthusiastically. "A real killer, man."

"Killer?" I stared at him. "Don't say that too loud, Mike. My folks hear that word and I'm dead."

He grinned. "It really doesn't mean what it says, Ron. Killer, when you're talking about a bike, means that it's a great machine. One of the best."

He sat on its seat, grabbed the handlebars, pressed gently on the starting pedal. Then he kicked it hard. Nothing happened, naturally. The battery was dead.

He got off it and looked it over with his expert eye. "Besides a battery you'll have to get lights, new fork springs, a new ignition, a new plug, and probably a new air cleaner. The water could have fouled that up, and probably a lot of other things, too. We should be able to save the chain."

Each part he listed was an X number of dollars I had to earn to get the bike in running order again. It could go into the hundreds, I thought. More than I would ever be able to earn in six months, let alone a few weeks.

Suddenly I didn't feel very good.

"Well, are we going to get with it, or just stand on our two feet stargazing at it?" asked Mike.

"Get with it," I said. But, get with what? What did he figure on doing?

"Let me take it to my place," he offered, answering part of my question. "We've got a bigger garage than you have, and I can start working on it right away. That is, if it's okay with you."

I stared at him, my heart pumping. "You mean that, Mike?"

"Would I say it if I didn't?"

I grinned. Suddenly the world was a whole lot brighter. "You're a pal, Mike. A real great guy."

"Stuff that sweet talk," he said, "and let's get this killer moving."

We pushed it to Mike's garage, where his Honda took up some space on one side of the two-car garage. His father's car sat on the other side.

There was more cleaning to be done on the mini. Under Mike's skillful direction he, Tony, and I removed parts, cleaned them, polished them almost to a shine, and oiled them when necessary. Ten o'clock rolled around before we realized it.

"I don't mind working on it all night," said Mike. "But our fathers will be on our tails if we don't call it quits for now. We'll get back on it tomorrow afternoon. I've got some errands to do in the morning, and I have to be at the theater tomorrow night."

"How long do you think it'll take before it'll be ready to run, Mike?" I asked anxiously.

"It depends. You'll have to get parts. A new speedometer, turn signals, horn, lights, shocks, a battery. The engine will need an overhauling. So might the clutch. One thing going for it — it wasn't sitting in salt water. That really would have ruined it."

I felt sick. The parts were going to run into money. And I could not just let Mike put a lot of his time into the bike without my giving him something.

He found a pad and pencil on the workbench and began writing. When he was finished he handed the top sheet to me.

"That's for a starter," he said. "Most of the parts were water-damaged. Best thing to do is to replace them with new."

I read some of the parts he had on the list. Shocks. Plug. 26mm carb. I frowned. 26mm carb?

I looked at Mike. "What's a twenty-six mm carb?" I asked.

"You *are* new, aren't you?" he said, grinning. "It's a carburetor with more trick to it than a nineteen-millimeter. This baby is already equipped with a quiet pipe, so you won't have to worry about too much noise bothering the neighborhood. Got it?"

"Got it," I said. But I wasn't sure I did.

# 4

The next morning I wrote up a Job Wanted ad.

Lawn mowing, shrubbery cutting, window washing, etc. Money needed to buy parts for minibike. Call 838-4441.

My mother had me cut the part about the bike. "It's nobody's business why you want the job," she said. "People will find out later if you want to tell them."

I stuck my wallet with a few bucks in it into my pocket, rode my bike to the newspaper office, and handed the copy to a young woman in the classified ads department. She counted up the words and said, "That's fine. It'll run for four days. If you want it to run longer, give us a ring."

"Okay," I said. I paid her and left.

The ad was in the paper late that afternoon. Mike, Tony, and I spent the afternoon working on the bike, quitting at four-thirty, since Mike had to clean up and get ready to leave for the theater. His hours were from five to ten.

Two days went by and I heard nothing from the ad. There were too many parents and kids doing their own lawn mowing, shrubbery cutting, and so on, I thought despairingly. I had visions of my little dirt bike sitting unusable in our garage forever.

But in reality the bike was getting in good shape, except for the parts that we had removed and that needed replacing. Mike was great. He could not have worked on it any harder if it were his own. I'm sure of it.

"What are you figuring on doing when you get out of school?" I asked him.

He laughed. "Fix motorcycles!" Then he got serious. "Oh, I don't know. I like fixing bikes, but I've been thinking about flying."

"Flying? You mean like for a major airline or something?"

"Right."

Mike had big dreams. But he was a smart kid. And a go-getter. I didn't doubt that he could make it.

On Friday afternoon, while I was at Mike's, my mother telephoned and said that someone had answered my ad. She gave me the person's number, and I wrote it down; I was so nervous I was afraid I'd forget it.

I rang the number and a woman's voice answered. "Hello? Perkins residence."

"H-hello," I stammered. "I'm Ron Baker, the boy who put the ad in the paper for a job."

"Oh, yes," she said. "Your mother said you would be calling. Can you come over here within the hour? Mr. Perkins would like to talk with you."

"Yes," I said. "Yes, sure. I'll be there, ma'am. Thank you. Good-bye."

I almost hung up when I heard her say, "The address is One hundred Summer Drive. It is on the north end of the lake."

"One hundred Summer Drive," I echoed. "Okay, ma'am. Thanks. I'll be there within the hour." I hung up.

The north end of the lake?

Suddenly the name, Mr. Perkins, hit me like a rock. Of course! He was the rich guy with the large, twenty-room house — maybe more — a four-car garage, and an acre of lawn!

What would he want of me? Didn't he have a gardener — a *professional* gardener — taking care of his lawn regularly? I shivered.

Maybe I hadn't made my ad clear, I thought. Maybe I should have said that I was only twelve years old. He probably thought I was in my late teens. Darn it, I should have made that clear with the woman who had called.

"I've got to go, guys," I said to Mike and Tony. "You wouldn't believe who answered my ad!"

"The President of the United States," said Mike, flashing his rows of teeth.

I smiled. "Not quite. Mr. Perkins. The Mr. Randolph Perkins, the richest guy in Ordell County."

"Wow! How about that?" said Mike. "Maybe he'll pay you enough to buy a new bike!"

"Or slam the door in my face when he sees that I'm just a kid," I said. "Look, you don't have to work on the bike any longer today. Why don't you quit?"

"I'll have to, anyway," replied Mike, looking at his oil-smeared hands. "It's almost four, and I have to be back in the mines again at five. Let us know in the morning how you made out. Okay?"

"Sure will," I promised. "But I think I already know."

Mr. Randolph Perkins was in his seventies. He was tall — one of the tallest men I had ever seen. His hair was white, bushy. His eyebrows were black. He was wearing sunglasses and carrying a cane.

I remembered having seen him once on the streets walking alone with his cane. I never knew who he was. Just another blind man, I had thought. I was stunned. I couldn't believe it. This was Mr. Randolph Perkins, the rich guy with that big, half-a-million-dollar mansion? The minute he heard me speak he'd boot me out of the house!

"Mr. Perkins," said the woman who'd let me in, as she introduced us in the huge, elegant living room, "this is Ronald Baker, the young man who had the situation wanted ad in the paper."

"Oh yes!" he said. "How are you, young fellow? I'm pleased to meet you, I'm sure!"

We shook hands.

"I'm pleased to meet you, too, sir," I said nervously.

I felt hollow inside, and out of place. I could see large pictures on the wall behind him, a brick fireplace, and a painting of a woman over the mantel.

"Come in, come in," he said. "Have a chair, young man. So you need a job, do you? Why?"

"Well — to purchase parts for a minibike, sir."

"Very interesting," he said, pointing his cane to a sofa as if he could see it. I sat down. He sat on a high-backed chair beside me.

"My man, Ollie, is ill," he explained. "Thinks he has the flu. He's my all-around maintenance man, but he won't be gone long, and I don't expect you to do everything he does, anyway. Mow the lawn, trim the shrubbery, take out the garbage. That's the kind of job you're looking for, isn't it?"

"Yes, it is."

"Good. How old are you?"

"T-twelve. I'll be thirteen in December."

He cleared his throat and leaned back. "Tell me about your minibike."

I looked at him. Why should he be interested in my minibike? I wondered. Anyway, I told him how I had found it, about Tony and me raising it out of the lake, and about Mike's helping me to get it into running condition.

"There are a lot of parts that need replacing," I finished. "That's why I need a job. My parents think that I should work for the money to repair it."

"You have wise parents," said Mr. Perkins. "I'd like to meet them sometime." He took a long-stemmed pipe out of one pocket, filled it from a small bag of tobacco he took out of another, and lighted it. Then he rose from the chair.

"Come with me," he said.

I followed him into an adjoining room. Just inside it I stopped, stunned. It was filled with bookshelves, pictures, and rows of trophies. An old rolltop desk sat against one wall.

But it was the pictures and the trophies that really caught my eye. Most of the pictures were of racing cars and motorcycles. And closeups of drivers.

Wow! So Mr. Perkins had been a motorcycle driver and a race-car driver, too! No wonder my reason for the job had interested him!

"By now I should think that the racing pictures have captured your attention," he said, smiling. "Right?"

"They sure have," I answered, my nerves tingling.

"I drove for thirty years, Ronnie," he explained quietly. "Both motorcycles and cars. I did everything. Climbed the steepest hills, competed in enduros, both in this country and in Europe. Then I began losing my eyesight. I had to quit."

"I'm sorry to hear that, Mr. Perkins."

"Well, it couldn't be helped. And I regret nothing. I led a good life, and enjoyed myself. I bought this big house, and for a long time had a party almost every weekend. Times change, though. Haven't had a party in five years. Frankly, parties lost their appeal. I guess I'm getting old."

He chuckled, and went back into the living room. I followed him.

"Well?" he said. "What's your answer? Would you like to work for me?"

I gazed at his dark glasses. I couldn't believe it. This was almost a miracle. "I — I sure would, Mr. Perkins," I stammered again.

"Fine. Will ten dollars an hour be all right?"

Ten dollars an hour? For mowing the lawn and cutting shrubbery? That was more than twice what I had expected!

"Anything you say, Mr. Perkins," I said, trying to hide my elation.

"Good. Do you have a social security number?"

"No, sir. I don't."

"You should get one. Might as well now as ever. You'll have to get one sometime. Then let me know the number, because that will have to be taken out of your check. So will your compensation insurance. Okay. Tomorrow is Saturday, and Genevieve — that's Mrs. Kennedy, my housekeeper — told me that the grass is beginning to get long. Can you start tomorrow morning? At eight o'clock?"

"I sure can, sir."

"Good."

Suddenly a male voice behind me said, "Hi, Uncle Randy."

I turned, and there on the threshold stood a tall, thin guy about eighteen or nineteen, dressed in khakis and a white sweater. His hair was blond and wavy, and looked as if he had just run a comb through it.

"Oh, hi, Mark," greeted Mr. Perkins. "Mark, this is Ronnie Baker. I've just hired him to work for me while Ollie is out with the flu. Ronnie, this is my nephew, Mark LaVerne."

We said hi and shook hands. But I noticed that he didn't smile, and that his hazel eyes were not quite as friendly as I would have expected.

# 5

I worked on Saturday morning till noon, then went back in the afternoon and worked till four. Mr. Perkins gave me my first paycheck and said he would expect me on Monday morning, at eight o'clock sharp.

I told him that my father was going to take me to the social security office early Monday morning to apply for my social security card, so would about nine be okay? He said sure.

Just before I started to leave, a snazzy, lemon-colored sports car pulled up into the long, curving driveway and parked in front of the house. Mark LaVerne stepped out of it.

"Hi, Mark," I greeted him pleasantly.

He didn't answer. He only waved. It was just a brief gesture, at that.

He doesn't like me, I thought. I wondered why. Was he jealous because I was working for his uncle? Did he want the job? Did he feel he was better than me because he didn't have to work?

I doubted it. I felt sure that it was something else. But what?

I rode away on my bike, feeling his eyes prodding my back. Suddenly I saw Tony riding down the street, heading toward me. I waited for him.

"Hi, working buddy!" he called, grinning. "You cleaning up?"

"In more ways than one," I said. I showed him the check. "That ought to buy me some parts. And I'm working Monday, too."

"No way, that's great!" he exclaimed, smiling.

I mentioned Mark LaVerne. "I don't think he likes me," I said.

"Why not?"

"I don't know. I have a feeling he might be jealous that I'm working for his uncle. But I don't know why he should be. Heck, if he's driving a sports car he should have all the money he needs."

"Don't worry about it," said Tony.

That evening Tony and I went to a bike store and I bought some of the parts that were on my list — a spark plug, battery, lights, bolts. They were all simple to install, but Tony helped me.

After our family's big dinner on Sunday, Tony and I rode our bikes to Turtleback Hill Dirt Track. There were races going on all afternoon, starting at one o'clock, with the minis racing first, and then the bigger-class bikes afterward. I wanted to see the minis especially, because that was the class I would be entering once I got my bike running and accumulated some experience under my belt.

Turtleback was about three miles outside of Ordell. Once my minibike was ready I'd have to get my father to cart it there, since riding minis on the streets wasn't legal. I had found that out.

Turtleback Hill was more than just a hill. It was a series of hills. The track went up and over them like a roller coaster, with trees and shrubbery in between. It was operated by a man named K. C. Jones, who owned the track and the land it was on.

Tony pointed him out to me as we went by an open tent. There was a long table under it with about half a dozen boys and girls standing by it, looking over a man's shoulder at a list he had in front of him. He was small and had a short haircut.

"His kid rides, too," explained Tony.

The place was crowded with riders, bikes, and bike enthusiasts. There was even a hot dog–soft drink concession stand.

We heard the final call for the first mini race, and got up to the fence near the starting line to watch. About twenty bikes were entered.

For a while the roar was deafening as each rider revved up his engine, warming it up for the race. Finally the starter fired the gun, and the bikes took off.

I felt my eyes bugging out of my head as I watched them head for the high hill. Then they climbed it, dirt flying from behind the rear tires as they clawed and gouged at the ground. I pictured myself in that crowd. One of these days, I thought.

"How long is the track?" I asked Tony.

"One and three-tenths miles," he said. "This will be three laps, I think."

After the bikes vanished over the hill we hurried over to another section of the track and watched the rest of the race from there. It was a three-lap race, all right, and a kid with a Honda 80cc won it.

We hung around and watched the other races. Lug Maneer and Skitch Bentley were entered in the 125cc's, but neither came anywhere close to winning their heat.

We finally left at five o'clock.

Early on Monday morning my father got my birth certificate and took me to the social security office, where I applied for my card. It was a good thing I had my wallet with me with my library card in it, because I also had to present an identification with my signature on it. It would take a while before I got the card, but what a feeling! I was almost a full-fledged member of the U.S.A.'s working class.

My father dropped me off at home, then drove on to work.

I rode my bike to Mr. Perkins's house. Ollie was still out with the flu. Recuperating, I imagined.

It was during the afternoon, while I was trimming the shrubbery, that I heard a soft sound behind me. I turned. It was Mrs. Kennedy with Mr. Perkins.

She smiled. "Ronnie, Mr. Perkins would like a chat with you," she said.

"Hi, Ronnie," he said cheerfully. "How are you doing?"

"Just fine, Mr. Perkins."

"Good. Okay, Genevieve. You can leave us gentlemen alone, now. And don't worry about me. I'll find my way back."

"And he will," she said to me. "All he has to do is turn his head until his nose points toward the kitchen."

"Genevieve, you talk too much," Mr. Perkins snorted. "Get on with you, will you?"

She winked at me, and left, her dress swirling about her skinny legs.

"Ollie won't be in till Wednesday, but I'd like you to give him a hand once or twice a week, if you don't mind," said Mr. Perkins. "Say Tuesday and Friday afternoons. That okay with you?"

"Sure is, Mr. Perkins," I said. I told him I had applied for my social security card, and he was glad to hear it.

"Well, how is your bike coming?" he asked.

"Great. It just needs a few more parts on it, and it'll be ready to go."

"That's fine. This boy — Mike somebody —" He

45

snapped his fingers as he tried to remember Mike's last name.

"Mike Franco," I said.

"Yes. He doing the work for you?"

"Most of it," I said. "He's got a bike of his own, and he knows bikes from one end to the other. He's really putting mine in good shape for me."

"Well, he'd better." He cleared his throat. "What are you doing right now?"

"Trimming the shrubbery."

"Time you cooled your heels a bit," he said. "Come on. Let's sit under that old oak tree for a while. These legs of mine will kill me if I stand on them much longer."

He pointed to a tall, ancient oak tree as if he could see it. We walked to it and sat down on a wood bench that was built around it. The seat was smooth and shiny. I had a feeling that Mr. Perkins had spent a lot of time out here, living in his dark world and breathing in the cool, fresh air that came blowing in from the lake.

"Genevieve says that you're doing a good job, Ronnie," he said. "I want you to know that I appreciate it."

"Thank you, sir."

"You know, you're the first kid I've talked with in years?"

"That's hard to believe, Mr. Perkins."

"Well, it's true. Since I've lost my sight I've hardly been out of the house. I've become a recluse. No kids come to the house because they have no reason to. Except the Boy Scouts and Girl Scouts now and then, when they're selling lightbulbs or cookies. Something to raise money for the cause. Genevieve handles that, anyway. I don't think I've talked with a kid in five years. You're the first one."

"What about your nephew, Mark LaVerne?" I asked.

"Mark? He just started coming around about a year ago. Just stays a few minutes — long enough to fill himself up with some of Genevieve's pies — then leaves. We never sit down and talk, as you and I are doing now. In a way, I hardly know him. But I suppose I know him well enough."

From what he said, and the way he said it, I figured that he wasn't too crazy about his nephew.

"He's borrowed some money from me," he went on, "when he's afraid to ask his father. And I always give it to him. Ten dollars. Twenty dollars. What-ever. He's promised he'll pay it all back someday, but I know he never will. Well, he's the only nephew I've got. Someday I hope he'll get a job and make enough money to buy what he wants."

"Hasn't he ever asked you for a job?"

Mr. Perkins laughed. "You kidding? Anyway, I wouldn't want him. Neither would Ollie. Ollie's told me so. Mark doesn't believe in picking an apple off a tree if someone would give it to him free." He chuckled. "Hear that? Involuntary poetry."

I smiled. "Pretty good," I said.

We sat there, talking a little more about Mark and his father, who operated a taxicab business. Then Mr. Perkins rose from the bench, saying that the seat was getting to him.

"Want your pay before you leave?" he asked me. "Do you need some more money right away to buy more parts for your bike? You'll have to get wearing gear, too, you know. A helmet. Padded pants. Boots. Gloves. You'll need them, and it all takes money."

"I know," I said. But I hadn't thought much about them. All I had uppermost in my mind was getting my bike to run.

"Come to the house before you leave," said Mr. Perkins. "I'll have Genevieve write you out a check."

"Mr. Perkins, you really don't have to. I can wait till the end of the week."

"Humbug," he snorted. "You heard me. Be at the house before you leave."

I was. And he paid me. For a rich guy, Mr. Perkins was the best.

When I rode away from the house on my bike I spotted a familiar car parked at the curb. It was Mark's lemon-colored sports car. And Mark was sitting in it. His face was in shadow, but I knew he was looking intently at me.

I figured on waving to him as I got closer. But as I approached, he started up the car and began easing it away from the curb. And then he gunned it.

# 6

My father, Tony, and Mike came with me to the sports store when I bought my riding gear — boots, pants, gloves, and a helmet with a mask. The complete bill came to much more money than I had, of course. But all it took was my father's signature for me to get a ninety-day credit. I thought that was great. I was sure I'd be able to pay up the bill by then.

By Wednesday evening the minibike was all repaired and ready to roll. I could hardly wait for Thursday to give it a spin.

But where could I go? It was illegal to drive minibikes on the sidewalks or streets. And our yard wasn't any bigger than a postage stamp. Even if I were able to drive around on it, the neighbors might complain of the noise.

Some fun, I thought. You didn't have to have a license, but you had to get out to the boondocks to ride. My excitement died like a quenched fire. For the first time in my life I wished we lived in the country. I'd have acres of land to ride around on then.

Well, maybe I could talk my mother into driving me and the mini to Turtleback Hill. And maybe Tony would consent to come along.

I suggested the idea to my parents. Right off the bat I could see that they weren't too crazy about it.

"Are you sure you can take your minibike there without asking for permission first?" my father wanted to know.

"I think so," I said.

"Make sure," my father said. "Do you know who owns Turtleback Hill?"

"Yes. K. C. Jones."

"Why don't you call him up first?"

"But I don't have to, Dad. I'm sure —"

He looked at me with those blue eyes of his that could become really stern at times. They were stern now.

"Do you mean to tell me that you can get on *his* property and drive around on *his* track without saying a word to him about it first?" he said. "If that's the case, every kid in the county with a bike would be there, tearing up the dirt."

"Well, I —" I hesitated, and maybe blushed a little. I hadn't thought about that. "Okay. I'll give Mr. Jones a call."

"It won't hurt," replied my father.

Two minutes later I came back into the room, my face a shade redder than it had been two minutes earlier. My father and mother looked at me.

"I can ride all right," I said. "But it'll cost me."

"How much?" asked my mother.

"Five dollars."

"That's what I thought," said my father. "Okay. Now that we have that settled, your mother can take you and your bike to Turtleback Hill."

I felt too sheepish to grin. "Thanks, Dad," I said.

I went over to Tony's house and asked him if he would like to come along with me to Turtleback Hill in the morning. He said he couldn't. He and Mike were going to Syracuse with their father to attend a boat show. Mr. Franco was a fanatic about boats. He was always buying and trading and looking. They invited me to go with them, but I didn't want to.

"Thanks, Tony," I said. "But the sooner I start riding the bike, the better."

The next morning my father helped me load the mini into the trunk of the car. It almost didn't fit. He had to tie the trunk door down with a wire to keep it from bouncing wide open.

My mother drove him to work. He was a mechanical engineer at a firm that manufactured boating equipment. Then she drove me to the track. Before we left him, my father offered some words of caution. "Be careful with that minibike. Keep your speed down. Learn all you can about the bike before you start turning it loose. Know what I mean?"

"Yes, I do, Dad."

"Okay. See you this afternoon."

My mother and I headed for Turtleback Hill and arrived there in about twenty minutes. K. C. Jones wasn't home, but his wife was. She said he had had to drive to Ordell for something, but that she was expecting me. I gave her the money for use of the track, then removed the mini from the trunk of the car.

"Where's the track?" my mother asked curiously, looking among the hills for it.

"About a quarter of a mile away," I said. "Down that road."

I pointed to a narrow dirt road that turned sharply to the left from the one we had come in on. It tunneled through a patch of woods, beyond which was the track.

"Don't you want me to drive you to it?" my mother asked.

I grinned. "No, Ma. I can ride this thing there."

I got on the Jonny Jo and kicked the starter. The engine sputtered, then died. I kicked it again, and it popped to life. I gave it throttle, twisting the grip on the right handlebar back and forth. The roaring noise sounded great. The feel of metallic power under me made my heart beat with joy.

I looked at my mother.

"Are you sure you'll be all right?" she said.

"I'm sure," I answered.

"Okay. I'll feel better if I wait here just to make sure you don't kill yourself. See you in about an hour, okay?"

"Sure, Ma."

Then she parked the car, and I headed for the track.

Just beyond the trees was an open field, flat as a pancake and surrounded by a wire fence. Bikers used it to practice on before they took to the track.

I rode back and forth on it for a while, getting the feel of the bike. The field was bumpy, rutted by rain and by hundreds of other bikes that had ridden here.

Then I drove through an open gate to the starting point below the first hill. It was the steepest hill of the track. I gunned the engine and took off, feeling the bike move under me so fast that it almost left me.

Hold it, man! I said to myself, and eased up on the throttle.

I might have climbed the hill if I had continued on. I don't know. But I turned and coasted back to the starting line, and tried it again. I didn't give it as much juice this time, just enough to get good motion. But the Jonny Jo bounced like a bucking bronco going up the hill, and got out of control. I tipped over, but just as I was rolling off the bike, I turned off the throttle and let the ground come up and meet me. My leg grazed the dirt and my left elbow took part of the shock as I felt an electric jolt shoot up my funny bone.

I scrambled to my feet, picked up my bike, and once more coasted back down to the starting point. I sat looking at that hill for a while, a great big monster waiting for me to challenge it again.

I wasn't angry. I wasn't disappointed. I enjoyed the challenge.

"Okay, baby," I said. "This time we're gonna do it!"

We didn't. We climbed farther up the hill this time, but I hit a bump that I hadn't seen, and once again the mini went one way and I the other. Fortunately, both the mini and I came out of it unscathed.

But now I decided to continue on instead of going back down to the starting line. I didn't want to waste most of the hour trying to climb the hill, although I realized that, in a race, climbing that hill meant an awful lot in determining the winner.

I rode around the track, taking it easy — remembering all Mike Franco and my father had told me. Neither one of them had warned me about the bumps. I had to find out about them myself.

The bumps. The skids. The quick acceleration the instant I twisted the throttle grip. It was a lot different from riding a bicycle. But a lot more fun, too.

I went around the track twice. The third time around I heard another sound, the roaring, loud-droning sound of another bike.

I didn't turn around. I could tell by the sound that whoever was coming up behind me was no amateur at bike riding.

The sound crept closer. A moment later I realized that there was more than one bike behind me. There were at least two.

Before I had more time to think about them, two motorcycles zoomed by, one on either side of me. Neither one of the riders looked at me. But I recognized their bikes, their helmets, their jackets.

They were Lug Maneer and Skitch Bentley.

Before I circled the track they came up behind me again, then up alongside of me, slowing down to keep abreast of me.

I glanced from one to the other, a gnawing fear growing in my stomach. Were they trying to scare me? Perhaps see me lose my cool and control of my bike? If so, they were beginning to succeed. My hands were getting slippery from sweat on the handlebars, and beads of sweat were dripping down my face.

Suddenly they both cracked a smile and waved at me. I waved back, smiling, too. A forced smile. Then they burst ahead, dirt flying from their rear wheels.

I circled the track once more, waiting for them to come up behind me again. But they didn't, and I wondered whether they had left.

There was a wood building close to the starting line. I remembered that its large windows had been open in the rear and front when Tony and I had been here at the races last Sunday. They were closed now.

I looked for Lug and Skitch, and for their bikes. I slowed the engine of my mini down and listened for them. I heard nothing.

I rode around the track a few more times, then saw a car drive in at the open gate. It was my mother.

Her face was a picture of utter gloom as I rode up to the car. "Oh, my!" she exclaimed. "You're so covered with dirt I can hardly recognize you! Are you all right?"

I grinned. I really felt good. "I'm fine, Ma," I said. "Know what? This baby rides like a charm."

"Now I know why they call it a dirt bike," she said. And she smiled.

# 7

Three times a week my mother took me to Turtle-back Hill, and I got to know the Jonny Jo like the back of my hand. There was a Sunday meet coming up and I wanted to be in shape for it.

I continued with my job at Mr. Perkins's place at least twice a week, putting most of my money toward the practice runs at Turtleback, the parts for the mini, and the riding gear.

I had finally met Ollie. He was in his sixties. He was no taller than I, but he had a bulging stomach, and his hair was snow-white.

On a sunny, pleasant day I helped him pick weeds from around the flower garden and the garage. Both sides of the garage were covered with vines of red and white roses, so pretty that I knew Ollie had taken a lot of pains in caring for them.

Before I knew it twelve o'clock rolled around.

"Oh, Ronnie," said Ollie. "I almost forgot. Mr. Perkins would like to see you before you leave."

"Okay," I said. See me? Why?

I washed at a sink in the garage, then went up to the house.

Mrs. Kennedy let me in and showed me into Mr. Perkins's study. He was listening to a taped recording of what sounded like a boxing match. When Mrs. Kennedy informed him that I was here, he shut it off.

"Hello, Ronnie," he greeted me, smiling.

"Hi, Mr. Perkins," I said.

"That's the Joe Louis–Jim Braddock championship fight of nineteen thirty-seven," he explained. "June twenty-second, to be exact. I knew them both. Great guys. Great fighters. But Joe was better. He kayoed Jimmy in the eighth, you know. I was there. I saw it from ringside." He grinned. "Listening to it is like seeing it all over again. Well, how is the work going, Ronnie?"

"Just fine, sir," I said.

He chuckled. "You get along all right with Ollie?"

"Oh, yes. He's a real nice guy. He said you wanted to see me."

"Yes. I'd like you to have lunch with Genevieve and me. We'd like the company, and she's cooked up a delicious meal and baked a pecan pie. Does that whet your appetite?"

"Sure does," I said.

"Good. It does mine, too. Come on. Let's go and see if she's lived up to all the good things I've said about her."

So I ate lunch with Mr. Perkins and Mrs. Kennedy. Ollie, Mr. Perkins said, always drove home for lunch. Breaks up the day for his wife, a lonely woman with an arthritic condition, Mrs. Kennedy added.

Mr. Perkins did most of the talking while we ate, reminiscing mainly on his days as a motorcycle rider and racer.

"I raced on the top courses in the world, Ronnie," he said, a faint, nostalgic smile on his lips. "Daytona Beach, Florida; Langhorne, P.A." That's the way he said it, Langhorne, P.A., not Langhorne, Pennsylvania. ". . . Dodge City, Kansas. And I raced with the best of them. Henne, from Germany; Wright, from U.K."

"U.K.?"

"United Kingdom. Oh, that Wright was good, all right. One of the very, very good drivers, Ronnie. So was Henne. And Taruffi, a driver from Italy I almost collided with one time. We were taking a corner side by side, and my front wheel hit an object. I don't know what it was. Must've been a stone. But it threw my bike off balance, and I skidded, almost running into Taruffi. I ended up last, and Taruffi first. After the race, I remember, he came over to me and asked me how I was. Then he bought me a drink. Oh, well, enough of this, Ronnie. I don't want to bore you about my motorcycling days. That was many years ago."

"You're not boring me one bit, Mr. Perkins," I said. "I really enjoy listening to you talk about your experiences."

"Thank you, Ronnie. You're a nice, kind boy."

"Better get going on your lunch, Mr. Perkins," said Mrs. Kennedy. "Or it'll be cold, and you won't want it."

"Hot or cold, you know I always clean up my plate, Genevieve," he told her. He smiled at me and started to eat again.

I hated to leave, but it was nearly one-thirty when I thanked them both and left.

I worked again on Friday, and Mr. Perkins paid me. He said that he expected me back on Tuesday, and I promised I'd be there.

Just as I left the house I met Mark LaVerne coming up the sidewalk. It was the first time I had seen him in almost three weeks.

"Hi, Mark," I said.

"Hi. What are you doing here? Hanging around my uncle again?"

"I have been working for him for quite some time," I told him.

His eyes turned hostile, and his jaw muscles hardened. I knew that he suddenly had some very unpleasant thoughts about me. I remembered what Mr. Perkins had told me about Mark and his father, and I wanted to leave. But he stood in front of me, blocking my way.

"Are you through here now?" he asked bluntly. "I mean, for good?"

"No. I'm coming back Tuesday."

His eyes seemed to get even more hostile, and I was afraid to think of what he had in mind.

"You know that my uncle isn't very well," he said.

"Outside of his blindness, he looks all right to me," I said.

"Well, he isn't. So I don't think you should be seeing him so much. Maybe not at all."

I stared at him. "Why not? I don't think that I'm making him feel worse by seeing him."

"Maybe you're not old enough to know what's good for him — and you," he said gruffly. "How old are you, anyway, Ronnie?"

"Twelve."

"See? Just a kid. Anyway, I hear you've got your bike all fixed. What else do you want money for?"

"To pay for my gear, and keep working out at Turtleback for races."

"Oh, yeah? You know what I think? I think that you think you have found a soft touch in my uncle, and you intend to squeeze every penny out of him that you can."

I glared at him. "What a rotten thing to say! I'm not asking him for any more jobs than I need!"

I started to press by him, anger burning inside me, but he grabbed my arm.

"Hey, hey! Wait a minute! I'm sorry. All right? I'm sorry."

I looked at him. He was smiling now, but it didn't seem genuine.

"All right," I said. Anything to get away from him.

"Hey, I happen to have a few bucks on me," he said, his tone completely changed, like night into day. "How about letting me spring for a couple of sodas?"

I thought about the invitation a second, and didn't like it. Even if he wanted to make amends for the way he had acted toward me, he still gave me the creeps.

"No, thanks," I said. "I've got to get home."

"You sure?"

"I'm sure."

"Okay. See you."

"Yeah," I said.

He stepped aside, and I went by him to my bike, which I had left standing against a tree. When I reached it, I looked back and saw Mark walking slowly toward the house.

Why was he so uptight about my working for his uncle? I thought. What wrong could he see in that, anyway?

# 8

I could hardly fall asleep on Saturday night. My mind was on Sunday's meet, on the tracks, and on the competition. But mainly on the steep hill. Would I make it, or would I spill and let all that practice go to waste? I could already hear the laughs certain people would get out of it if I did.

Sometime after midnight I fell asleep. I knew it was that late because I heard the big clock in the living room bong twelve times.

The next morning my mother's call got me out of bed. I was half-asleep as I dressed, pulling my clothes on only from force of habit.

I didn't feel like eating. My stomach just wasn't up to it.

"You had better get something into your stomach," my mother said, "or you'll be so weak by the time you race you won't be able to twist your throttle grip. Have a bowl of cereal. Maybe it'll scatter away those butterflies and you'll be able to eat more."

I had the cereal, but it didn't do much about scattering away the butterflies.

My father was sitting across from me, a faint grin on his face. He had not shaved yet this morning, and he looked like a friendly hobo.

"Feeling nervous about what you're going to do is normal," he said. "But if you want to be in minibike meets, you'll have to make the break sometime. All those kids you'll be competing with had to go through the same thing. It's another price you have to pay to do what you want to do."

I suppose he was right. But that didn't help to scatter the butterflies, either. I guess it was something I had to live with. For a while, anyway.

I couldn't believe the crowd that was already there when we got to Turtleback Hill. The parking lot before you entered the gate was already half-filled. When we stopped at the gate and paid our fees, the girl who gave my father the tickets looked at me.

"You competing in a meet?"

"Yes."

"You had better get a move on if you want some practice," she said. "It's almost ten o'clock, and the first meet starts at eleven-fifteen."

I looked toward the track where the loud, mixed roaring sounds of bikes were coming from, and got a glimpse of about six bikes bunched together as they came sweeping around a curve, dust and gravel spraying from their wheels.

"Where do I sign up?" I asked nervously.

She pointed toward a mobile trailer that was parked close by.

"There, where you see that kid," the girl said.

A canvas roof had been placed in front of the trailer, under which a couple of people sat at a table. A kid about my age was talking to them.

"Thanks," I said.

My father drove the car in and parked it in front of a row of trees where over half a dozen cars were already parked. He helped me unload the Jonny Jo. I wheeled it to the trailer and signed up in the senior mini class.

"One of your parents has to sign, too," the woman who was handling the entry blanks said.

I must have looked surprised, because immediately her suntanned face broke into a smile.

"Gee, I hope you brought one of them with you," she said. "Or a legal guardian, even. You're not allowed —"

"Oh, my parents came with me, all right," I informed her. "I just didn't realize that one of them had to sign, too. That's all."

I called my father over, and he signed his name on the entry blank.

"Thank you," the woman said to him, smiling. "And here is Ronnie's number. One twenty-one. It's like a bib. Just slip it over his head and onto his shoulders. And paste this sticker on his helmet." She handed him a sticker with my number on it. "Now give me the entry fee and we'll be all set. Oh, you had better get in your practice, Ronnie. You have until eleven o'clock. The meet starts at eleven-fifteen."

"I know," I said. I waited for my father to lay the bib over my shoulders, showing the number on my chest and back. Then he pasted the sticker onto my helmet.

"I haven't seen you before," the woman went on, her eyes fastened on me. "Is this your first meet?"

"Yes."

"I hope it's the beginning of many more," she said pleasantly. "Good luck, Ronnie."

"Thanks," I said. "I think I'll need it."

The man sitting next to her cut in, "Before you do anything else, you have to have your bike inspected, Ron, old boy."

"Oh?" I looked at him. He had a stubble of beard that was almost as long as his very short hair. I had hardly recognized him. It was K. C. Jones, the track owner. "Oh, hi, Mr. Jones. Who does that?"

I felt a prickle of fear course through me. Suppose my bike didn't pass the inspection?

"I do that," he said. He sprang up from the table at which he was sitting — a pile of papers in front of him — and started to examine my bike from end to end.

71

"Looks like a lot of new parts on it," he observed. "Did it yourself?"

"No. A friend helped me."

"Whoever it was did a nice job."

"Mike Franco," I said. "Maybe you know him."

His face lit up. "I sure do. That boy knows what he's doing. He's also a darned good rider. He'll be here today."

"I know," I said.

The inspection didn't take long. "Well," he said, when he was finished, "your bike's okay, Ron. Good luck, and have fun."

I looked around at my father and mother. I don't know whether it was pride or concern that I read on their faces. Maybe a little bit of both.

"Well, son," said my father as he put out his hand. "This is it. I don't know what else to say, except good luck."

We shook hands. "That's all I need," I said.

"And the same from me," said my mother. "I'll keep my fingers crossed, too."

I wheeled the Jonny Jo toward the wide gate that led to the starting point. From the corner of my eye I spotted a dark pair of pants and a cane, and my heart sprang to my throat. Mr. Perkins! I suddenly thought. I stopped in my tracks and looked up.

But, in a flash, I saw that it wasn't Mr. Perkins at all. The man didn't even look like Mr. Perkins. It was just the dark pants and cane that had briefly caught my attention.

As I started by him, he flashed a warm smile at me. "Hi, buster," he said. "Nice bike you have there."

"Thank you," I said.

I went by him, still thinking about Mr. Perkins, and the stories he had told me about his racing days. I didn't think I'd ever meet another man as interesting as he was. Next to my father came Mr. Perkins in my list of great men I knew personally. I admired and liked him. I really did.

I entered the starting gate, started the engine of my bike, and let it warm up by twisting the throttle grip back and forth. I looked at the steep hill in front of me and felt a lump crawl up to my throat. If I didn't make that hill during practice, I might as well disqualify myself.

I sat there a minute, telling myself that I had to make it. A positive mental attitude is important. I had to get myself in that frame of mind, or I'd be a dead duck.

After a while I felt ready. With the engine in first gear, I took off. The bike almost left me sitting there on the dirt as it sprang under me like a live animal. I hung on, and plowed up the hill, the noise of the engine roaring in my ears. The bike bucked and bounced, and a couple of times it skidded to the side so much that I almost lost my balance and fell. But I managed to keep it upright, using my feet to balance it when I felt it leaning over too far. Little by little the Jonny Jo edged forward, dirt and gravel crackling against the inside of the small fenders.

At last I reached the top. From there it was smooth sailing. Well, maybe not smooth. But it was far less grueling than that first climb.

I rode around the track a few times, quitting just after an announcement was made that all riders clear the track.

Outside of the starting gate I saw a couple of bright faces that gave me a morale boost. Tony and Mike Franco. Mike was wearing his riding gear — leather jacket and pants, and high buckled boots — and carrying his helmet.

"Hey, you ride that baby like a pro," Mike said.

"Sure, I do," I answered. "I wish you'd get a mini, too, Tony. I'd feel better with a buddy on the track."

Tony shrugged. "Don't worry about it. After today you'll pick up a lot of new friends."

"Especially if they all leave me eating their dust," I said.

They laughed.

"I'm thirsty," I said. "Want to share a soda with me?"

"Why not?" said Tony.

"You two go ahead," said Mike. "I'm going to sign up."

Tony and I had a soda at the concession stand. We had hardly had a couple of sips of our drinks when a girl's voice announced over the P.A. system:

"All riders competing in the junior mini please get to the starting gate at once!"

I almost dropped my bottle on the counter. "Wow! Already?" I cried.

"Hold it," Tony said, grabbing my arm. "You're in the senior mini, aren't you?"

I relaxed. "That's right," I said, my heart pounding. "I guess I'm nervous, all right."

We walked to the fence and watched the junior minis race. The kids in this meet ranged in age from seven to ten years. And the way they rode their bikes was something. Those little guys had guts.

Both Tony and I rooted for a real small kid who must have just reached his seventh birthday. He had trouble making the hill and was the last one up. But he struggled hard after that around the S-curves and hills and wound up in fourth place.

Our meet came up next. Tony wished me luck. Then my mother, father, and Mike came over and wished me luck, too. I figured that if luck had a lot to do in winning, I should come out near the top.

I headed for my bike, and was within a dozen feet of it when I saw two guys examining it from a couple of feet away. I stared in surprise. One was Mark LaVerne. The other was a rider, about my size, wearing number 111.

"Hi, Mark," I said. "I didn't know you were interested in bike races."

"I am in this one," he said. He started to turn away, then said over his shoulder, "One way or another, Ron, I'm going to make you stop seeing my uncle."

He nudged the kid with him and they walked away. But I didn't miss the smirk that came over the rider's face first.

I stood there awhile, frozen by Mark's statement. If I had ever heard a threat, that was one. What did he figure on doing? I couldn't even guess. Unless he had that kid, Number 111, in his plans.

I would just have to wait and see.

I got on my bike, started it, and rode it through the starting gate. The engine sounded a little rough, and right away I wondered if the guys had tampered with it. I throttled it loudly a few times, and it cleared up. I took a glance over my shoulder and saw Mark talking to his friend, who was mounting his bike.

It turned out that the kid was in the same race as me. He was one of the six other riders lined up beside me. I tried to brush the thought of him out of my mind. After all, how could he be a threat to me in a race? Seconds later I began to feel more nervous than ever as crazy thoughts flooded my mind. Suppose my engine conked out before I reached the hill? Or suppose I spilled before I got halfway up?

I tried to forget those fears, and glanced over my

shoulder at Mike, Tony, and my parents. They waved to me, and I waved back.

"Okay, riders!" yelled the starter, his gun raised. "Get ready!"

Our engines were humming. My heart was pounding. This was it, I thought.

*Bang!* went the gun, and we took off. Up till now I had never sat close to more than one roaring engine. My own. Now there were seven in all, and the sound was something like the roar of an airplane.

We headed for the hill, reached its base, and started up. My bike hopped like a wild rabbit as we climbed, my rear end off the seat as often as it was on. Fear gripped me that I would never make it. That I would spill any minute. Or that my bike would break apart.

**9**

**W**atch it!"

The yell came from the rear to my right. Like a nut I glanced in that direction and almost wiped out.

The kid who had yelled was about two yards behind me. I recognized him immediately. Number 111. I could see his face and eyes through the plastic glass of his helmet. They were filled with a fierce determination, the strong desire to get in front of the pack. And to scare me, too, in the bargain.

Anyway, I maintained my balance. And I didn't move over for him. Gradually he crept ahead of me, then got in *front* of me. You rat, I thought. But by the time we reached the summit he was at least two lengths ahead of me.

Going over the top, I saw that there were already a couple of riders who had made it before me. But I wasn't tail-end Charlie. There were two others trailing me.

I glanced ahead again, and saw that 111 was about three lengths ahead of me now, and gradually increasing his lead.

I stepped up the speed of my bike. At the rate he was outdistancing me, I figured that he'd be at the finish line while I was starting my last lap. We had five laps to run.

In a few moments he was out of sight. I didn't look for him. You shouldn't look around when you're racing. You just make sure that no one's in front of you that you might run down.

For a while two other riders and I were about even. The three of us clung practically neck to neck as we swerved around the S-curves and negotiated the hills and valleys at a crazy speed. I don't know whether we were fighting for second place or what. I had no time to think about that. Nor did I care. I just wanted to ride, to get my bike to go as fast as it could and not take a spill. I wasn't thinking about winning. I was sure I had no chance to win. But I didn't want to lose, either.

Uppermost in my mind was just the fun of racing my bike.

We arrived at the area where the snow fence separated the crowd from the track. The crowd was just a blur as we whizzed by them. But I could hear their yells, and from the corner of my eyes I could see many of them jumping and waving, their jackets and blouses showing all the colors of the rainbow.

I sensed their attention upon me, and suddenly I wondered where I stood in the meet. Fourth? Fifth? Or was it last?

Soon we completed one lap.

Lap two was as grueling as the first. A rider took a spill far ahead of me, got back on his bike, and rode on. By then I had gained several lengths on him, and within the next few seconds I was even with him.

I thought I might gain on him going down the next grade, for I seemed to do better going downhill. Instead, it was the reverse. He pulled ahead of me. But I kept him in sight, using his back as a target. His number was 189.

We finished lap two, started lap three. I still had 189 in my line of vision, although every once in a while he would disappear for a few moments going down a grade.

It was when we were about halfway through the lap that I heard a bike coming up behind me. We were approaching an S-curve, and I hoped I'd get there before he'd try to pass me.

Then I heard the rider yell, and I didn't need a second guess to know who it was. He rode up beside me on my left side, so close to me he could have touched me if he stretched out his arm.

"Move it, Baker!" he yelled as he edged closer to me.

"Keep away from me, you!" I yelled back.

Up ahead, not twenty feet away, was the S-curve. Terror gripped me as we both came up on it, side by side. Then, fearing that we'd collide while making the turn, I pulled away from him, but accelerated so I wouldn't lose too much ground.

The Jonny Jo responded with more power than I intended it to. It roared ahead and struck a hard mound I didn't see in time, wrenching the grips out of my hands. The front wheel twisted, the bike rolled over, and me with it. I hit the ground on my side and rolled over a couple of times to avoid being struck by the bike.

Darn you, 111! I thought. Quickly I got back on my feet, saw a couple of riders roaring up fast to my left — well out of the danger zone — and ran to my bike. I throttled down the engine, then lifted it back on its wheels, climbed up on the saddle, and took off again.

I was scared stiff that something might have been damaged on it. But the bike rode as well as it had before. And, except for a slight pain in my right shoulder, I felt okay.

But the spirit had gone out of me. I suddenly didn't care whether I would finish the meet or not. Mark had put Number 111 up to it. There was no doubt about it.

As I rode near the crowd I thought I heard someone yelling my name. But the voice was almost drowned out by other screaming voices, and the roar of the engines.

Yet it perked me up. It made me want to go on and not quit. The heck with you, Mark! I thought. I'm going to ride to the finish!

Lap four was over. As we went into lap five I had practically forgotten about my spill. I drove fast, but more carefully. I just didn't want to take a chance of spilling again.

Somewhere during the lap Number 111 passed by me again. It might have been the third time he had done so. I don't know. You can't watch every single driver as he whizzes by.

At last I saw the checkered flag drop as I flashed by the finish line. Several others had finished before me. I thought for sure that I was last.

But no. Another bike came trailing behind me. It was, I realized, the last one. So I had finished next to last.

A lousy finish, I thought. But I could have done better if I hadn't taken that spill. If Number 111 hadn't interfered.

I rode slowly off the track and met my parents, and Tony and Mike.

"Hey, you rode that bike like a real vet," exclaimed my father. "If it weren't for that spill, you would've done real well."

"I struck a hard bump," I said. "I accelerated on a curve to pull away from another bike, and didn't see it in time."

I could have told them about Number 111 getting in front of me, but I didn't. It just might sound like another excuse.

"You did okay," said Mike.

"How are you?" my mother asked worriedly. "Did you hurt yourself when you fell?"

"No. I'm fine."

"Sure, you are," she said, a knowing glint in her brown eyes. "You could have a bone sticking out of your shoulder and you'd say you're fine."

I smiled. "There's no bone sticking out of my shoulder or anyplace else, Ma," I assured her. "I'm fine. Honest."

A voice started to blare from the loudspeaker.

"Attention, ladies and gentlemen! The winner of the senior minibike meet is Glen Garner! Coming in second place was Jimmie Smith! Third place, Tom Pullin! Fourth place, Dick Fleming! Fifth place, Biff Daniels! Sixth place, Ronald Baker! And last, but not least, Richie Spencer! Congratulations!"

A cheer exploded from the crowd.

I saw a handful of guys go over to a rider and shake his hand. Among them was Mark. The rider was Number 111, Glen Garner, winner of the race.

As the guys walked away from him, all except Mark, I saw Mark take out his wallet and hand Garner some money.

How about that? So Garner was Mark's pigeon! He was paid to do what he had done!

I turned away, boiling mad. He had done his dirty work without anyone else noticing it!

A man broke through the small crowd and headed toward me. It was Mr. Jones.

"Hi, Ron," he greeted me. "You did all right, in spite of that fall. You okay?"

"Yes, I am, sir. Thanks."

"Good." He looked at my father. "Hi, Mr. Baker. I saw you at the front desk" — he chuckled at the term — "when you signed in with your boy. I'm K. C. Jones, the track director."

"Oh, yes," my father acknowledged as they shook hands. "And you're also the owner of this track, aren't you?"

"Right." K. C. Jones's eyes sparkled. "It was inevitable. After my kid bought a bike and rode around the place, some of his friends started to come around and ride, too. After watching them for one whole summer, I thought that I might as well turn it into a real track and have it open for every kid within a certain radius. Now it's one of the best tracks in this part of the country."

"You should be commended for that," said my father. "It isn't everybody who would turn a fat chunk of land into a motorcycle track."

"For the kids, Mr. Baker. It's for the kids. Of course I'm making a few bucks on it, too." Again his eyes shone. "Frankly, it isn't the choicest piece of land I've got," he admitted. "It's hilly, as you can see, and covered with a lot of shrubs and trees through most of the inside of the track. Now and then I get out there and cut down a tree for the fireplace. Comes in handy."

"Sure does," said my father.

We got around to talking about points. K. C. Jones figured it out that my having come in sixth, in a category of seven participants, earned me six points.

"We follow the AMA amateur point system," he explained. "From six to twenty participants, first place earns twenty points, second place ten points, third place nine — and so on down to eleventh place, which earns one point. So Ron earned six points."

"And if there are more than twenty participants?"

"Between twenty-one and thirty, and with each additional ten participants, the points increase. After several meets the points are tallied and the top points-earner cops the winning trophy."

"I see. So a kid doesn't always have to win first place to cop that trophy, does he?"

"Righto. As a matter of fact," K. C. Jones looked at me with a glint in his eyes, "with any amount of luck, Ron still has a chance."

"Oh, sure," I said, laughing. "I might as well wish for a million bucks."

"Well, say a thousand, anyway," K. C. Jones said, flashing slightly stained teeth. "But don't despair. That was just the first heat. There will be another one at one-thirty for the senior mini. Each class is running two heats, so you'll have another chance of piling up your points."

Just then someone yelled his name, and he excused himself. After he left, I looked at Mike.

"Supposing," I said, "just supposing I do have a chance, like he said. How many meets would I have to enter to qualify for that trophy?"

Mike and Tony burst out laughing together.

"Sorry I asked," I said.

"No, *we're* sorry," said Mike. "We didn't mean to embarrass you, Ron. Anyway, the number of meets isn't always the same. It's determined by a committee sometime during the season. But this meet happens to be the third of five, and there are two heats in each meet. Believe me, you would have to be darned lucky to come even close to the top. K. C. Jones has so much on his mind, I don't think he realized it when he said you'd stand a chance."

I felt a mixed reaction when I heard that. It might have been fun, I thought, to see how many points I could acquire if this were the first of five meets instead of the third.

I could hardly wait, though, for the next heat. One-thirty would be a long time coming.

**10**

**W**e watched the other heats. Mike, competing in the 125cc class, came in a close second, winning fifteen points in a heat with twenty-four riders. That gave him a total of fifty-three so far, having come in first and fifth in the earlier two meets. He had as good a chance as anyone to win the trophy when the meets were over.

We had a light lunch — hot dogs, potato chips, and sodas — and one-thirty rolled around at last.

I was less worried than during the first heat, except for that hill. I'm sure it worried every other rider, too. I could tell by the way they looked at it. But it was there, and it had to be climbed. If you didn't make it, you were out of it. It was that simple.

At last the gun blasted, and we took off. My little Jonny Jo flew up that hill like a real live pony. Granted, not a smooth *riding* pony. She bounced, galloped, and tried hard to unseat me. But I hung on. And soon the top of the hill was there in front of me. And then it was behind me.

The toughest trial was over. I had conquered it.

Running the laps was easier than during the first heat. But it was easier for the other riders, too. I didn't know where I stood at the end of the first lap. Nor at the end of the second one. I was more anxious to keep my bike under control than to bolt full speed ahead, taking a chance of having a mean spill.

Finally it was over. I was pooped. Every inch of my body ached.

And, good thing, too, Glen Garner hadn't tried any monkey business.

The announcement of the winners came over the loudspeaker. Tom Pullin, who had come in third in the first heat, came in first. I waited anxiously for my name to be announced. Biff Daniels was second, Glen Garner third, Ronald Baker fourth.

Ronald Baker! That was me! I had come in fourth! Two better than in the first heat!

"Well, son," said my father, gripping my hand and smiling broadly, "you've moved up a couple of notches. Fourth place gives you eight points, a total of fourteen in all for the two heats. Congratulations."

"Hi, honcho!" Tony cried, as he came running up. "You're riding like an old pro, man!"

I grinned tiredly. "Right now what I would like is a big glass of water and a hot shower."

"Those," chimed in my mother, "you'll get at home. Come on. Let's get cracking."

We loaded the Jonny Jo into the trunk of the car and drove home.

It wasn't long after I had had my glass of water and taken a shower that I got a phone call from Mr. Perkins.

"Ron, my boy!" he said, a jovial ring in his voice. "I just heard the bike reports over the local station. You came in sixth in the first heat and fourth in the second. That's good riding!"

"Thanks, Mr. Perkins," I said. "But there were only seven of us in the meet."

"Don't kid yourself," he replied. "Even with only seven, sixth and fourth *is* something. Did you enjoy it? That's the important thing."

"Oh, yes, I did, sir. I enjoyed it very much."

"Good. That's what I like to hear. Okay, Ron. Keep up the spirit. And say hello to your family for me."

"I will, Mr. Perkins. Thank you."

I hung up. Can you beat that? I thought. He took the time to call me up and congratulate me!

"Who was that?" my mother asked.

"Mr. Perkins. He heard the report over the radio and wanted to congratulate me."

"Even if you came in sixth and fourth?" My mother smiled. "He's a thoughtful gentleman, indeed."

"He is really that, Dorothy," said my father. "He likes you, Ron. You've made a friend in Mr. Perkins."

"He's a great guy, Dad. I'm glad that I've got him for a friend, too."

I guess I could consider Mr. Perkins almost as close a friend as Tony. But it was that friendship that bothered his nephew so much that he had paid a rider to scare me in a race.

I got a surprise on Wednesday when my mother drew my attention to an item in the evening paper.

"Read that," she said. I did.

It was an announcement of an eight-mile cross-country test race for minibikes. The race was going to take place on Saturday morning at ten o'clock, starting at Millers Grove. That was less than ten miles from here. Applicants had until five o'clock Thursday evening to sign up.

The surprise was that my mother had taken the time to read the article and tell me about it. Up till now I had thought that she just had a lukewarm interest in the sport.

"That sounds good, Ma," I said. "Would you mind if I entered it? It would be something different."

"It certainly would," she agreed, then shrugged. "Well, I'll leave it up to your father. That's more along his line, anyway."

"Where is he?" I asked. "I haven't seen him around for the last hour or so."

I heard the kitchen door open, then my father's firm footsteps.

"Speaking of the devil," said my mother, smiling.

My father stared at her. "Who? What?"

I grinned. "Hi, Dad," I said, and mentioned the article about the cross-country test race. "I'd like to enter it. Can I?"

"What's a cross-country test race?" he asked, frowning. "A test to see how the bikes stand up?"

"That could be. I don't know. I can ask Mike."

"Well, that won't be necessary," my father said, heading for the sink. "I suppose it would be an interesting experience. Yes, you may enter it."

He ran the water and washed his hands.

I know that my eyes must have lit up like flashbulbs. "Thanks, Dad."

"Now, it's my turn," he replied, turning off the faucet and drying his hands. "I'd like to go scuba diving for a while at Pumpkin Head Lake, and I wouldn't mind some company. How about it?"

I smiled. "Why not?"

We left half an hour later, and dove for almost an hour near Honeymoon Point — some three miles from where Tony and I had found the minibike — then came home. My father hadn't been in the water for nearly a month, and I knew he missed it. Working a lot of overtime at his job left him too tired to do much else.

He drove me to Market Street immediately after arriving home from work the next day, and I signed up for the cross-country. He had to sign, too. I paid the entry fee out of my own pocket.

I asked the man I paid my fee to what a cross-country test race was, and his answer was exactly what my father had guessed it to be. It was to test the maneuverability and durability of the bikes, although an entrant didn't have to restrict his bike to the rules if he didn't want to. Since my bike was a restored piece of equipment, I thought that the test wasn't a bad idea.

When we got home, my mother said that Ollie had called. There wasn't very much to do for Friday so I didn't need to come for a few days. I went to bed feeling disappointed about not working but relieved in a way. The scuba diving had left me pretty exhausted and I kept thinking about the cross-country, the kind of terrain I would be biking over. Rough paths, rocks, ditches. No doubt "cross-country" meant exactly that.

I soon fell asleep. But something during the night woke me. I opened my eyes wide and stared into the not-too-black darkness of the room. A light on the street corner about half a block away was just powerful enough to reach my window and turn most of the objects in the room into pale outlines.

I heard the sound again — like the sharp squeak of a door — and I sprang up to a sitting position.

*Somebody was in our garage!*

Heart pounding, I got out of bed and tiptoed to the window. Very carefully I drew back one side of the curtain and peeked out. I was able to see the garage, and the window that faced me. I stood there a few seconds, holding my breath. The garage was absolutely dark.

Then — there was a flash of light! As if a flashlight had been turned on!

I released the curtain, ran out of the room, and almost collided with my father.

"Dad!" I whispered. "Somebody's in our garage!"

"I know!" he whispered back. "What do you think I'm sneaking around with a flashlight like this for?"

I followed him down the stairs. *Squeak! Squeak!*

"Sounds as if these steps need some nails driven into them," my father grunted softly.

I never realized before how incredibly loud the squeaks sounded.

We reached the kitchen, and very carefully approached the door, me trailing my father by a step. He unlocked it, turned the knob, and pulled the door open.

Just then I heard what sounded like a thud. It came from the rear of the garage. My father moved, and then I, for the thud sound was followed by that of running feet.

In a second we saw the intruder. He was sprinting at an angle across the back of our lawn to the next.

My father turned the light on him, catching a flash of a pair of dark pants and a dark windbreaker.

We started after him, my father leaping off the porch with me at his heels. I didn't know whether Dad had put on his slippers or not, but he sure ran as if nothing bothered his feet. I did, too.

The intruder hurdled the short fence separating our yard from the next, then ducked and disappeared around the house. By the time my father and I got around the house and to the street, he was nowhere in sight.

"Darn it!" my father exclaimed.

We listened for running footsteps, but heard nothing.

"Well, no sense in standing here —" my father started to say, when we heard a motorcycle start up in the distance. "Well, there he goes. Come on. We might as well report this to the cops, then check to see if he took anything."

We returned to the garage, where my father checked a rear window. The bottom sash was wide open.

"So that's how the jerk got in and out," my father said. "He cut a hole in the window, reached inside, and unlocked it. A real pro."

"I wonder if he took anything," I said.

"Come in the house and get the key to the garage door," my father said. "I'll call the cops."

We went in and I got the key. I was slightly chilly, so I slipped on a light jacket. While my father dialed for the police, I went out, unlocked the garage door, and flicked on the two overhead lights.

My minibike was there in the corner, where I had left it. But it was lying on its side now. And I remembered distinctly having left it upright.

# 11

**F**ear struck me as I ran toward my bike. I glanced over it, looking for missing parts. They all seemed to be there.

I was about to breathe a sigh of relief when I spotted something that told me that we had not interrupted the thief a minute too soon. Two screws were loose on the carburetor. About half of their threads were showing.

"So that's what he was after," I said out loud.

"What?" said my father, just entering the garage.

"The carburetor," I said. "He had loosened two screws on it. I guess we stopped him just in time."

My father came closer and knelt beside the bike with me. "Are you sure nothing else was touched? Here. Let's get it on its wheels."

We lifted it together. I gave it a thorough check this time, and now saw a gap that I had missed seeing the first time.

"He took the spark plug," I said.

"If that's all he took, you're lucky. Let's make doubly sure, though. The police will want to know."

We both gave the bike a more thorough examination, but couldn't find anything else missing. I went to the workbench, and was about to pick up a wrench to tighten up the loose screws on the carburetor when I noticed an empty space beside it.

"Uh-oh," I said.

"What is it?"

I glanced over the workbench, looking for a special tool.

"Did you let anybody borrow those locking grip pliers?" I asked.

"No. I don't think so."

"Well, they're gone."

"The punk," grumbled my father. "I guess he knew a good thing when he saw it. But he'd better not let anybody see them."

"Because your initials are on them?"

"Yes."

"But what if he grinds them out?"

"That would only make it look more suspicious."

A flashing blue light shone through the garage windows. Seconds later a car stopped out front.

"Man, they sure got here fast," noticed my father. "Let them in, Ron."

I went to the side door and opened it. Two uniformed policemen got out of a police cruiser that had stopped in front of the driveway.

"Hi," I said.

"Hi, there," one of them answered. "Are you Baker?"

"Yes. Ron Baker. My father's in here."

They entered the garage, introduced themselves as Officers Wilkins and Conley, then listened to my father and me explain what we had heard and seen. The second policeman began taking notes on a pad.

"Did either of you have a good look at the person?" Officer Wilkins asked.

"We just saw him running across the lawn and leaping over the fence into the next yard," replied my father. "I had my flashlight shining on him, but it wasn't strong enough for us to really get a good look at him."

"Was he short? Tall?"

"Medium, I'd say. That's the best description I can give of him. But he was agile, and fast. I'd say he was in his late teens or early twenties."

"Did you see his face?"

"No."

"How about you, Ron?"

"I didn't, either," I said. "He was running away from us, and didn't look back once."

"Okay. Anything else you can add to what you've already told us?"

My father mentioned the missing grip pliers, and his initials that were engraved on them, P.R.B.

"Why don't you call the lab, Tom?" Officer Wilkins said to his colleague. "Maybe they'll be able to lift some prints."

Officer Conley nodded, folded his pad, and walked out of the garage. I stood rooted like a statue, listening and watching. This all seemed like a wild dream. I felt that I would wake up and find that none of this had happened.

My father looked at me. "Maybe you should go back to bed, Ron," he said.

I stared at him. "Can't I stay till the men from the lab come?" I pleaded.

I had seen fingerprints "dusted" for on television, but never in real life. There was something suddenly very exciting about this.

"Okay," said my father. "I suppose you've earned it."

The lab men — two of them — arrived in about ten minutes. They dusted parts of the minibike and the window sill, then laid plastic films over the dusted areas, lifted them off carefully, and placed them in envelopes.

"Any good ones, Bob?" Officer Wilkins asked one of the men.

"We lifted one off the minibike that looks fairly clear," the man called Bob said. "I'm afraid that the others are too smudged to help."

The lab men left.

"If the print they got matches up with any of those we have on file, we'll have our man," said Officer Wilkins confidently. "He could be the same guy who's successfully pulled off a series of similar robberies during the last six or seven months."

Something popped into my mind. It must have shown in my eyes, because Officer Wilkins said, "What's the matter, Ron? I say something that got you thinking?"

"Well — I don't know."

"What do you mean you don't know?"

I shrugged. "I would just be guessing," I said. "And I might be wrong. Real wrong."

"You think you might have an idea who committed the robberies?"

I didn't know what to say.

"Look, Officer Wilkins," my father intervened quietly. "Why don't you let me talk to my son privately about this? If he knows anything that would help you, I'll let you know. Can we leave it like that?"

He smiled. "Sure, Mr. Baker. It's pretty late, anyway. We had better get going and let you two go back to bed. Good night."

The policemen left. I looked at my father. I wanted to hug him tightly, but all I said was, "Thanks, Dad."

He smiled and patted me on the shoulder. "Come on. Let's turn out the lights."

We turned them out, locked the doors, and went into the house. My mother was in the kitchen, waiting for us with anxious eyes.

"I began to wonder if you two were coming back in, or were going to wait till daylight," she said. "Who was that other crew that showed up?"

My father told her. Then, nervously, I waited for him to ask me who I thought it was that was committing all the robberies Officer Wilkins had mentioned. But he didn't. He just looked at me, smiling faintly. He wasn't pressing me, and I was glad. I was getting pretty tired and sleepy, anyway.

If the thief were either Lug Maneer or Skitch Bentley, the fingerprint that the lab man had lifted would be all the police would need.

It wasn't till the next evening, after my father came home from work, that he asked me the question. "We might as well get it over with, Ron," he added. "It will be on your mind, and mine, too, if we don't."

I took a deep breath. "I could be wrong, Dad. It's just a guess, like I told Officer Wilkins."

"Okay. Who are you guessing it could be?"

"Either Lug Maneer or Skitch Bentley."

His expression didn't change.

"You're not surprised?" I asked.

"No. Because those guys had crossed my mind, too. But, as you said, it's just a guess, and guesses don't work. Anyway, both Lug and Skitch have kept their noses clean ever since they got into trouble almost a year ago. I doubt that they would risk their reputations again — and a term in jail — by committing a series of small robberies."

"But the robberies are all connected with minibikes or motorcycles, Dad," I reminded him.

Somehow, I wasn't altogether convinced that neither Lug nor Skitch was involved.

"No matter," said my father. "Lug and Skitch are innocent, until proven otherwise. And you had better remember that."

"Yes, sir," I said. "Are you going to call Officer Wilkins and tell him what I said?"

"No. Suspicion isn't enough, Ron. I think it's best that we let the cops handle it." He smiled and patted me on the shoulder. "Forget it, and start concentrating on that eight-mile cross-country test race."

# 12

Saturday was one of those days I could have slept till noon. I might have, if it weren't for the cross-country test race. My clock said eight, but the pale light in the room made it look more like five.

I rolled out of bed, pulled aside the curtain, and saw puddles of water on the street.

"Oh, no," I groaned.

I put my nose up against the window and peered out to see if it was still raining. It wasn't. But the sky looked as gray as ashes.

I got to thinking of the race. What a muddy mess it could turn out to be. Maybe they'll cancel it, I thought.

*Oh, no! Please don't cancel it! I want to ride in this cross-country! I want to see what it's like! I want the experience! And, especially, I want to ride in it so that I can tell Mr. Perkins about it! He'll be proud of me! I know he will! Even more so than my mother and father, because he knows what it is to ride a bike! Even a little dirt bike like mine!*

The thought of the race excited me. Eight miles! Wow! And probably every inch of it was over rough terrain.

I went to the bathroom, then dressed and walked into the kitchen. My father and mother were at the table, having toast and coffee. Soft music was coming from the radio on the counter.

We exchanged good-mornings.

"Not such a hot day for a cross-country race, is it?" my father said.

"I just hope it won't rain any more," I said.

"What would you like for breakfast?" my mother asked me.

"Nothing," I said.

She smiled. "How about a couple of eggs and toast?"

I shrugged. "Okay."

I hardly remembered her frying the eggs, or me eating them. I just suddenly came out of a trance and saw my empty plate and glass in front of me.

"For someone who wanted nothing at first, you did a pretty good job of making your breakfast disappear," my mother said, smiling.

"That's good," said my father, reaching for the morning paper that was on the counter. "You need a big breakfast for what you're going to do."

"Who's driving me to the track?" I wanted to know.

"We both are," replied my father. "So don't dillydally. Better start getting into your outfit."

I got off the chair and headed for my room. All at once my knees felt weak, and my stomach felt as if I were going to upchuck everything I had eaten. I hurried to my room and flopped down on the bed.

I heard footsteps, then my father's voice. "Ron, are you all right?"

"I'm better," I answered softly. But I still felt woozy.

"What happened?" my mother asked worriedly. "Did you feel like throwing up?"

"Yes. But just for a minute. I'm better now."

"Would you rather stay home?"

"No, Ma. I'm going to that race. I'm okay."

Then I turned over and socked the pillow with my fist. Darn! I thought. Getting sick before a meet! Nothing could be more dumb.

Half an hour later my father and I loaded up the Jonny Jo into the trunk of the car and we all drove to Millers Grove, a town so small it wasn't even on the map. We arrived there in fifteen minutes. The post office was in the same ramshackle building as the grocery store. A single, rusty gas pump stood out front.

It wasn't hard to find the field where the meet was to start. A huge sign next to a dirt road read: CROSS-COUNTRY MEET, SATURDAY, AUGUST 8, with an arrow pointing toward the field beyond. Already dozens of cars were parking in the field, and riders with their bikes were all over the place.

We unloaded the Jonny Jo, and I wheeled it toward a tent where another huge sign read: SIGN-UPS HERE. The ground was a little soft from last night's rain, and crisscrossed with bike tire marks. I wondered how the entire track would be.

I signed up, then saw Mike about a dozen yards away, leaning against his bike and cleaning his helmet shield. Tony was with him.

I went over to them, catching them by surprise.

"Hey, Ron!" Mike exclaimed, smiling. "Good to see you! Haven't seen you all week. Been riding a lot?"

"Not since the last meet," I said. I looked at Tony. "When are you going to break down and buy a bike, buddy?"

He grinned. "When the prices go down."

"You've got a long wait," I said.

At last the announcement came over the P.A. system: "Attention, riders! Please listen carefully! This meet will be comprised of three classes! In the first will be the minis, which will include the sixty-five cc's through the eighty cc's! In class two, eighty-five cc's through the one twenty-five cc's! And in class three, the two hundred fifty cc's!

"The track is seven point seven miles long, and is marked at every half mile by a red flag. So don't panic if you get off the track and think you're lost. Also, there are marshals along the way, each one equipped with a walkie-talkie to keep each other, and us here at the main tent, informed in case anything happens to you or your bike. Again we extend our thanks to the Van Atta Volunteer Fire Department for their courtesy in standing by with two of their ambulances, one here at the starting line, the other at the finish line.

"Okay! All the minis please get in position at the starting line! Hurry! Let's move it!"

"See you guys!" I waved to Tony and Mike.

"Good luck, pal!" said Tony, making a victory sign with two fingers.

I started the engine of my bike and rode to the starting line, which was simply an imaginary line in front of a snow fence. Louder and louder grew the noise as more bikes moved into position. There were eight in all. One of them was Glen Garner. I should have known. What dirty trick would he try to pull today?

In a minute the starter dropped his flag, and we took off.

This start wasn't bad. Nothing like Turtleback Hill where you had to grapple, gnaw, and struggle your way up before you reached the top and settled down to more level riding. Relatively level, that is.

We crossed a field that was about a quarter of a mile long, then broke through a row of pine trees into the next field. Keeping on the track was easy; it was covered with tire ruts, and the weeds were all matted down.

I dared to look around and saw that I was riding third. The rider in the lead was about four lengths ahead of me, the second about two. The race only just started! How could they do it?

I gave the Jonny Jo more throttle, and felt the power take hold. The bike jumped, bounced, and I almost lost my grip. I had a hard time keeping my feet on the pegs, and the wheels out of the ruts. I tightened my hold on the handlebars, and concentrated my attention on the route in front of me. Wow, I thought. If the route was this bad now, imagine what it would be like after we rode over it!

A long hill loomed ahead of us, sparsely dotted with trees, stumps, and bulging rocks. An arrow pointed out the driving direction for us. Near it stood a woman wearing a large straw hat and speaking into a walkie-talkie. Our first marshal, I realized.

The ground was rock-hard on the hill, but there were ruts we had to cross. I slowed down and lost precious seconds by the time the hill was behind us and we entered another field, this one even worse than the one we had left. The track led over one small hill after another, with patches of bare rock washed clean by the rain. With the dirt we were throwing up, they wouldn't be clean very long.

I gained on the second-place rider, who seemed to have closed the gap slightly between him and the guy leading the pack.

We were neck and neck for about a hundred yards. Suddenly I saw him swerve and lose control of his bike. A second later something dashed across the track in front of me, and in a frantic effort to avoid hitting it, I twisted my front wheel. I had a blurred glimpse of a rabbit before it scooted off to my left. I tried to straighten out the wheel, but by then the momentum had swung my bike too far off balance, and I felt myself going over. Helpless, I let go of the handlebars and rolled over with the fall.

Quickly I stopped the roll, scrambled to my feet, and remounted my bike. It had stalled. I lifted it, started the engine, and got it moving again. I cursed the rabbit, and glanced at the other rider to see how he had made out.

He was still on his wheels, and back in second place by a comfortable margin. As a matter of fact, two other riders had pulled ahead of me, taking advantage of my spill.

We passed a second marshal, another woman, accompanied by a couple of teenaged girls who waved enthusiastically at us.

Then, about a quarter of a mile farther on, I sensed something very strange about my front wheel. It was getting harder and harder to steer, and now I realized why.

The tire was going flat!

Nuts!

I couldn't go on. And it would be stupid for me to try to drive it the next four or five miles, even at a reduced speed. I would ruin the tire for sure.

I killed the engine, got off the bike, and stood there, angry at the tire, and at the rabbit that had chosen to cross my path at just the wrong moment. I was sick, frustrated.

I started to push the bike back to the marshal and the two girls. But, before I reached their post, the girls came running forward, wondering what had happened.

"Flat tire," I explained, trying to control my emotions.

"Oh, too bad!" one of them moaned.

"I'll say it is!" said the other. "Take it easy. We'll push it to the marshal for you."

"Oh, I can do it," I said.

"Listen," the shorter of the two looked at me sternly. "We're not weak, and this bike isn't that heavy. This is our job. Let us handle it. Okay?"

I gave in. Why not? I thought. "Okay," I said.

They pushed the bike to where the marshal stood. Immediately the woman started to speak into her walkie-talkie, saying something about me and the bike. Then she fastened her large brown eyes on me. "What's your name? Are you okay, and what happened to your bike?"

I told her, and she related the information over the walkie-talkie.

"Someone will be here in a little while and pick you up," she said to me. "The road is just a few hundred feet from here." She looked more closely at me, frowning. "You've been on this cross-country track before, haven't you? You look familiar."

"No. This is my first time in cross-country. But I was in the meet at Turtleback Hill last week. Maybe that's where you saw me."

She smiled. "Right," she said. "I'm so sorry for you. What a rotten beginning, isn't it?"

"Yeah," I said.

"Well, there will be other cross-countries. You'll have better luck next time, I'm sure."

Fifteen minutes later someone showed up from behind the trees that shielded the road from the track.

It was my father.

**13**

**W**hat happened?"

He was alone. I assumed that my mother had remained in the car he had left parked on the road.

I told him about the rabbit, and the spill. My tongue was dry. My lips felt like sandpaper.

He looked at my jacket, pants, and boots. I looked at them, too. They were a mess.

"Are you okay otherwise?" my father asked. "No hurts from the spill?"

"No."

"You're sure? Because I can drive you to the ambulance where a medic can fix you up in no time."

"I'm sure, Dad," I insisted.

I wasn't only frustrated. I was embarrassed.

Deep inside, I had wanted my father to be proud of the way I raced. I had hoped to finish at least in the top five. In a meet of eight participants, even fifth would not have been bad for a beginner like myself.

But to drop out because of a flat tire? Sure, it was an accident. But why did it have to happen to me on my first cross-country?

"Well, let's go," my father said, taking hold of the handlebars. "But better brace yourself when we get to the car. Your mother might want you to ride on the hood."

I didn't laugh.

When we arrived at the parked car I saw my mother in the front seat, staring at me as if I were a ghost.

"You're covered with mud," she said. As if I didn't know it.

"That's what worries him," said my father. Smiling, yet.

"What do you mean?" she asked.

"He means, Ma, that with all this gunk on me, you might not want me to ride in the car," I explained.

She shrugged. But a faint smile came to her lips, and I knew that I wouldn't have to worry about riding on the hood. Anyway, I had a better idea. I looked around to be sure no one could see us, then took off my jacket, pants, and boots and laid them in the trunk beside the bike.

"How's that?" I said, bounding into the rear seat.

"Fine," said my mother. "But I can just see what the inside of my washing machine will look like once I get your messy clothes into it. Heavens! It seems that somebody would have enough sense to cancel an event like this when it's so muddy. But, of course, what do I know about such things?"

"Very little," replied my father softly. "But you'll learn. We'll all learn. Right, Ron?"

"Right," I said.

He started the car and got it moving. Somewhere in the distance I heard the roar of the bikes, the sound growing loud as the bikes reached a summit, and fading away as they dipped into a valley. A sadness overwhelmed me. I sure wished that I could have at least finished with them. Even coming in last would have been better than not coming in at all.

✤　　✤　　✤

We arrived in Ordell, and presently were on our street.

"Uh-oh," said my father as we came within sight of our house. "We've got company."

The "company" was a police cruiser. It was parked in front of our house. For a moment I couldn't see anyone in it. Nor was there a policeman in sight.

A moment later two officers came walking out of our driveway, and I recognized them as Officers Wilkins and Conley.

Now what? I thought. For a minute I forgot that I was practically naked.

They stepped aside as my father drove up into the driveway. We got out of the car. I asked my father for the house key, and he handed it to me. I ran to the back door, unlocked it, and went in. Then I ran into the living room and peeked out around the edge of the curtain through the window at the cops and my parents. Officer Conley was talking, but I wasn't able to hear him. I looked at my father and mother, hoping to tell from their facial expressions whether the cops' news was good or bad. But their backs were to me. And the cops' facial expressions didn't tell me anything at all.

It wasn't until after they had left and my parents came into the house that I learned what happened.

"The fingerprints that the lab men had lifted from the windowsill of our garage did the trick," explained my father. Then he lifted a tool he was holding. The missing grip pliers. "And my initials on these pliers helped, too," he added.

Immediately Lug Maneer came to my mind. Or was it the other half of the pair? Skitch Bentley?

"Who was it, Dad?" I asked, anxiously.

He looked at me. "A young man from the other end of town," he replied quietly. "An Edward Bruning. Ever heard of him?"

I stared at him, and felt awfully funny.

"No," I answered, my voice so soft I barely heard it myself. "Never."

"Neither have I," said my father. "Anyway, he has a record of thefts, and already has been jailed once. He'll have to appear before a judge, and we may have to testify. Messy business, but maybe after this penalty he'll think twice before pulling another robbery."

I found his eyes searching deeply into mine, and I knew what he was thinking.

"Well, I'm glad it wasn't someone we knew," he said. "For some reason, there seems to be a difference. What do you think, Ron?"

"I'm glad, too, Dad," I said. I guess I had misjudged Lug and Skitch. People can change. "It just goes to prove what you said. That a person is innocent until he's proven guilty."

He patted me on the shoulder. "It's not what I said. It's what our justice says. Now, why don't you go back out there, bring in your mud-plastered stuff so that your mother can get them in the wash, then take a shower and get dressed? Have you got enough energy left to do that?"

I smiled. "I think so," I said. "As a matter of fact, I'll go one better than that. I'll wash them, too."

"Well . . . good!"

I ran out and hauled in the load. What the heck, Ma deserves a break once in a while.

After lunch I hosed down the Jonny Jo. Then my father and I took off the front wheel. A gash about three inches long was in the tire. I felt a lump form in my stomach, because that meant that I had to buy a new one. And they don't go for peanuts.

"When is your next meet at Turtleback?" my father asked me.

I thought a minute. "Two weeks from today," I said.

"Well, you definitely need a new tire. Have you any money left in your savings?"

"Not much," I said.

"You'll need a fair amount for a tire. Even for a twelve-inch." He paused. "Well, I suppose I can give you whatever more you need to buy one."

"Thanks, Dad."

But suddenly I got to thinking of working for Mr. Perkins. Ever since the first day I had worked for him it seemed that he was the first person I would automatically think about when I needed money for my minibike. Anyway, I didn't want to impose on my parents if I could help it. My racing that minibike was a fun sport, not a necessity.

"I'll call up Mr. Perkins first, Dad," I said. "Maybe Ollie can use some help for a few days."

My father smiled at me. Tiny suns danced in his blue eyes. "Okay, Ron. But let me know if he can't."

"I will, Dad."

It wasn't till late that afternoon that I telephoned Mr. Perkins's home. Mrs. Kennedy's soft, high-pitched voice answered. "Hello? Perkins residence."

"Mrs. Kennedy, this is Ronnie Baker," I said.

"Ronnie! Well, bless you! We haven't seen you for a spell."

"I know. How — how is Mr. Perkins?"

There was a moment of silence. I suddenly felt that something was wrong. "He's not well, Ronnie," she replied finally in a subdued voice.

"He isn't? What's wrong with him?"

"Well, he became ill about four or five days ago, and has been in bed most of the time since then," she explained softly. "Usually he hates to follow his doctor's orders. He's stubborn as a mule, at times. But this time he obeyed like a child."

"Oh, wow," I said.

I didn't know what to do. I couldn't tell her that I had called up mainly to ask Mr. Perkins for a job. It didn't seem the right time to ask.

"He's talked about you several times, Ronnie," Mrs. Kennedy went on. "Just yesterday he said that he hadn't heard from you in a while. He's been wondering how you're making out in your minibike meets."

"Do you — do you think it's okay if I stopped in to see him for a minute?" I asked. "Or is he too sick to have company?"

"I'm not sure. Look, I'll go and ask him. Hang on for a minute."

While she was gone I told my mother the sad news about Mr. Perkins. She frowned with worry. "Oh, dear. I hope it's not serious," she said.

"It sounds like it is," I said.

Mrs. Kennedy was back. "Ronnie, he told me to tell you that he's never too sick to see a good friend. He'll be glad to see you anytime."

"Oh, good. Is this afternoon okay?"

"This afternoon will be just fine, Ronnie."

"I'll be there, Mrs. Kennedy," I said, and hung up.

"What are you going to do?" my mother asked.

"I'm going over to see him," I said. "He's been asking about me."

I went to the bathroom, washed, then changed into clean clothes. I told my mother I was leaving, got my bike, and rode off. It was about a quarter of five by then.

Some ten minutes later I pulled up into Mr. Perkins's driveway and got something of a surprise. Ollie, who usually quits at four-thirty, was still there. He was near the garage, cleaning a tool that looked like a paint scraper. Which it was. He'd been scraping the old paint off the garage.

"Hi, Ollie," I greeted him. "Working late, aren't you?"

He smiled. "Well, Ronnie, ol' kid! Long time no see! And, yes, I am. What are you doing here at this time of day?"

"I came to see Mr. Perkins. Mrs. Kennedy said he's sick."

"Sick, he is," said Ollie, wiping off the tool and laying it on a piece of cloth. His forehead creased. "Did she call you and tell you he's sick?"

"No. I called."

"You looking for work, Ronnie?" he asked, smiling.

I grinned weakly. I hoped he didn't think I came around only for a job. "To tell the truth, yes. I got a deep cut in my tire this morning when I rode in a cross-country, so I have to buy a new one. But I'm not going to say anything about it now to Mr. Perkins. I won't do that."

"You won't have to," said Ollie. "Just come in at eight o'clock Monday morning. I've got plenty of work for both of us. I'll tell Mr. Perkins about it, myself. Go on," he said, waving me toward the house. "I'm sure he'll be very glad to see you. By the way, I am, too."

I parked the bike and walked up to the house. My heart beat like a drum as I knocked on the front door.

# 14

Mrs. Kennedy answered my knock. She looked pale, and there were tiny red lines in her eyes. I had a feeling that she wasn't getting the sleep she needed. Doing housework and cooking meals was plenty enough to do. But when you had to take care of a sick person during the day — and night, too — it would take a lot out of you.

"Come in, Ronnie," she invited. "It's so nice to see you."

"It's nice to see you, too, Mrs. Kennedy," I said.

She took me into Mr. Perkins's room. It was huge. Besides the bed, there was an armchair, and a bookcase filled with books. I wondered why Mr. Perkins would still want them around since he was blind.

He was lying in the large bed with the pillow propped up high so that he was almost sitting up. He had on his dark glasses, and was facing me as if he could actually see me.

"Hi, Ronnie," he greeted me, even before I had a chance to greet him.

"Hi, Mr. Perkins," I said, and went over and shook his hand. "I'm sorry to hear you're sick. I wish I had known about it. I would have stopped in earlier."

He smiled. He looked paler than I'd ever seen him before. The lines in his face seemed deeper, making him look ten years older.

"Well, I have thought about you. You've been very much like a son to me, you know. Even though I don't see you very often. And when I say *see*, Ronnie, I mean exactly that. Because I have a picture of you in my mind." He chuckled. "I had Genevieve describe you to me one day."

I laughed. "I guess she told you I wasn't very big."

"She didn't tell me that you were very small, either. About medium, she said. Which makes you about my size when I was your age." He sighed. "I don't know what happened to me, Ronnie. My doctor says it's nothing serious, that I'll get over it in a few days. Well, it's been almost a week now. And I feel all drained out."

"Oh, you'll get better, Mr. Perkins," I tried to assure him. "I'm sure you will."

"Now you sound like my doctor and Genevieve," he said. "But what else can a real friend say under these circumstances? Right?"

"Mr. Perkins, you're just too smart," I said.

"Smart, but unhealthy. And that's the problem, Ronnie. What good is being smart if you're too sick to get out of bed?" He made a swipe at the air with his right hand. "Oh, shoot. Let's cut out this dull chatter about sickness. Nothing is more depressing. Tell me about your racing."

The statement hardly left his lips when I felt my face get hot as fire.

"I entered a cross-country this morning, Mr. Perkins. But I didn't finish."

"You didn't? What happened?"

I told him.

"Is that all? You got a flat?" He laid his head back and laughed. "That's no big deal to feel bad about, kid! It happens to the best of 'em! Listen, if you knew how many big names lost races because of flat tires, your head would swim. That's part of the game, Ronnie. It's not always all cake and frosting. A chain can break. A piston can pop. A clutch can go. It's a guessing game what can happen next. But the more you ride the more you learn, and the less these things will happen. All of it won't disappear for good. No machine is built that way. And as long as it's a human being who rides them, there are going to be problems.

"But that's the nature of the animal, Ronnie. That's what makes it more fascinating." He laughed again, a little harder than before. "All in all, it's the best sport in the world, Ronnie. You're free as a bird. You can go as slow as you like, or as fast as you like. You're sitting on that little two-wheeler, gripping her handlebars, and speaking to her through your hands, your feet, and your whole body. There's nothing in the world like it, Ronnie. Nothing."

His face was glowing, and he was smiling broadly. He was happy talking about his favorite sport, and I felt good that it was me he was happy to talk with about it.

"Just remember not to let it drag you under," he went on. "Make it your body, but not your soul. Know what I mean? *You* be its master. Don't let *it* master you. And don't let a loss discourage you so that you want to throw in the towel. It's the losses that strengthen you, that make you a better rider. And a better man. Take it from me, Ronnie, your old friend, Randy Perkins. I've been through the tunnel — two or three times."

He was silent awhile. Then he took a handkerchief from under his pillow and blew his nose.

I thought about telling him that Ollie had asked me to come to work Monday, but again I felt that this wasn't the time to talk about work.

He stuck the handkerchief back under the pillow and adjusted his glasses. "When's your next meet, Ronnie?" he asked.

"Two weeks from today," I said.

He put out his hand. "Ride it good and clean, Ronnie," he advised. "Don't worry about taking first or second. Just ride it good and clean. The places will take care of themselves. Okay?"

"Okay, Mr. Perkins." I knew the handshake meant that he would like us to quit the conversation for now. And I could see that he was more tired now than earlier, and wanted to rest. "It was real nice talking with you. Good-bye, sir."

"Take care, Ronnie."

Something came over me then, and I put my arms around him and hugged him. And he hugged me. A big lump rose in my throat.

After a while we broke apart and I turned away, tears burning my eyes.

I started to head for the door when I saw someone there, standing directly in front of it. It was Mark LaVerne. For a moment I wondered if he were going to move, if he would mutter a greeting.

But he just looked at me with a pale light in his eyes. He didn't say anything, and I didn't, either.

I waited for him to step aside. He did. I walked out of the room, said good-bye to Mrs. Kennedy, and left the house.

On Monday morning I was at Mr. Perkins's place promptly at eight o'clock. I helped Ollie remove the paint from the garage. It took us most of the day. We finished it the next day, and started painting.

We talked about different things — about the minibike meets, about school, and about Mr. Perkins.

"Is he feeling any better?" I asked Ollie.

"I don't know, Ronnie," answered Ollie. "I haven't seen him any more than you have these last two days."

Which wasn't at all.

"I'll see Mrs. Kennedy later on and take a look in on him," he went on. "Maybe you —" He didn't finish. The sound of a car driving into the driveway stopped him. His eyes swept past my shoulders. "Uh-oh," he said. "Guess who's driving in."

"Mark LaVerne."

"You guessed right."

I didn't turn to look, but presently I heard footsteps approaching.

"Hi, guys," Mark greeted us, in a friendlier tone than I had ever heard from him before. "How are da Vinci and Michelangelo coming?"

"They're not," said Ollie. "If you remember your

history, Leonardo da Vinci died in 1519, and Michelangelo in 1564."

"Sorry I asked," Mark said glumly. Then he laughed. "I didn't know you were so well informed on painters, Ollie. Congratulations."

"You learn something every day," replied Ollie, not missing a stroke with his brush.

"I suppose you're here, Ron, to weasel some more bucks off my uncle," Mark said. "For a new tire, isn't it? I heard you got a flat in the cross-country."

My face turned hot. I looked at him for just a second, and felt like whipping a brushful of paint into his face.

"Hold it, Mark," snapped Ollie, his piercing eyes fastening on Mark. "What's the idea embarrassing the kid like that? You should have more sense. And he's working for that money. He's not 'weaseling' it. Why don't you turn around and get the heck out of here? Okay?"

I turned and went back to my painting, my hand shaking, and thought hard about what Mark had said as he snickered and walked away.

"Don't let him bother you none, Ronnie," said Ollie. "He's just jealous that his uncle has taken a liking to you, that's all. He's just a no-good spoiled brat, that's all he is. You know why he's been dropping in so often since Mr. Perkins has been sick, don't you? I hate to say this, and if it was to anybody else except you, I wouldn't. But he's got a mind that maybe Mr. Perkins is on his last legs. And he wants to make sure that Mr. Perkins doesn't forget him in his will. He isn't fooling this codger none. Not one bit he isn't."

I smiled at him. "Who said you're a codger, Ollie?" I said. "And how come you know so much about painters?"

Ollie grinned at me. "Knowing those dates was easy," he said, chuckling. "Portrait painting is my hobby. So is reading biographies of famous painters. Takes the dullness out of an otherwise dull evening."

I laughed, but Mark's stinging comment still lingered. Suddenly I wished I was about five years older. I think I would have landed a solid punch on his kisser.

**W**e finished painting the garage at about three o'clock.

"As soon as we get these brushes cleaned, we'll go and see Mr. Perkins a minute," said Ollie.

He worked on the brushes while I covered the paint cans and cleaned them. Then, using turpentine, we rubbed off the spots of paint we had on our hands, washed our hands thoroughly with soap and water to get rid of the odor, and walked up to the house.

Mrs. Kennedy answered Ollie's knock. When he told her that we'd like to see Mr. Perkins for a few minutes, she said she would check on him first. She did. A few seconds later she came back and told us regretfully that he was asleep and she didn't think she should wake him up.

"You're right, Mrs. Kennedy," agreed Ollie. "We wouldn't want you to do that. Suppose we popped in about ten tomorrow morning? Will that be all right?"

She smiled and nodded, but I could see that there was genuine concern in her eyes. "That is a good time," she said. "He's been having a cup of tea about then. I'm sure that he'll be glad to see both of you."

"Okay. We'll see you in the morning, Mrs. Kennedy," said Ollie.

I almost didn't go to work the following morning. I wouldn't have, if my father hadn't knocked on my door and asked me if I had forgotten about my job.

"I'm not going, Dad," I answered through the closed door.

He cracked it open and poked in his head. "You're not what?"

"I'm not going," I repeated.

He stared at me. "Why not?"

I hated to explain why not, but I knew that he wouldn't leave for his job if I didn't give him an explanation.

"Mark LaVerne stopped at his uncle's house yesterday, and came over to talk to Ollie and me. But he came over mainly to see me. I'm sure of it."

My father frowned. "What did he say to you?"

I felt a twinge in my stomach. "He said, 'I suppose you're here to weasel some more bucks off my uncle.' I would have busted his face in if I were any bigger, Dad."

"If you were bigger, he might not have said it," replied my father.

"Maybe not. Anyway, Ollie shut him up. He said that Mark should have more sense than embarrassing me like that. And that I was working for my money, not weaseling it."

"Ollie was right. And I think you're not by staying in that bed. Ollie expects you, doesn't he?"

"Yes." I hesitated, and wondered if I should tell him something else about Mark. That he was responsible for my taking a spill in my first race. But I didn't. Maybe eventually I would, but not now. "We were going to see Mr. Perkins for a few minutes this morning, too," I said.

"All the more reason why you had better get your tail out of that bed. And you had better snap to it," he said emphatically. "It's getting late."

A grin flashed across his face, creasing the corners of his blue eyes. He pushed the door open wider, stepped into the room, and came over and kissed me on the forehead, something that he didn't do very often. I liked it.

"I love you, son," he said.

"I love you, too, Dad," I answered.

Then he was gone, and I got up and dressed. Somehow, I felt much better.

There were times when I felt that I was the luckiest kid in the world for having parents like my mother and father. This was one of those times.

Mr. Perkins was ready to meet Ollie and me at ten o'clock. Mrs. Kennedy showed us to his room, then left.

He was in bed, propped up against two pillows. His hair was combed and he was clean-shaven. But you could tell that he hadn't been out in the sun in quite some time. His face was almost white as paper.

"Well, hello, Ollie. Hello, Ronnie," he greeted us jovially, extending both of his hands. "I'm so glad you stopped in."

We shook hands, and I got the feeling that he could really see us.

"Hi, Mr. Perkins." Ollie smiled. "You're looking fine."

"Well, I'm holding my own," said the old-time racer. "And how about you, Ronnie? Got a new tire for your bike yet?"

I hesitated for just a second before I answered him. I hoped he didn't notice it, but I think he did.

"I'm going to buy it this week, sir," I told him. "The first chance I have to get to a store."

The smile faded, and he was quiet a moment.

"Something wrong, Mr. Perkins?" asked Ollie wonderingly.

"Oh, no. I was just thinking. Couldn't you smell the rubber burning?" He chuckled. "Ollie, take Ronnie to the sports store this minute, and get him the tire he needs for his bike. You can drive it home for him before you bring him back to work. And have Ernie bill me. Got that?"

"Got it, Mr. Perkins," grinned Ollie.

I stared at him, then at Mr. Perkins. "Sir, I'll pay for that tire."

"No, you won't. It's a gift. A bonus on top of the pay you will be getting. Come here, Ronnie."

He extended his hands again. I stepped closer to the bed and put my hands in his. They were trembling a little. I looked at his eyes through the dark glasses.

"I just had to touch you, Ronnie," he said. "Since I can't see, touching is the next best thing. Of course, I'm lucky to have the senses I do. And my memories. Would you like to hear more of my motorcycle days? Not now, of course. But sometime later, when I'm better and feel more like, well . . . bragging. Would you?"

"I sure would, Mr. Perkins."

"Good. I'll let you listen to some of those old fight records I have, too. I'm not asking Ollie, because he has already heard them. Okay. Take him to get the tire, Ollie. A bike ain't worth a plugged nickel sitting in a garage not doing anything. It's got to have exercise, just like a person does. See you again, Ronnie. And thanks for stopping in."

"Thanks again for the tire, Mr. Perkins."

"My pleasure," he said.

Ollie purchased the tire, billing it to Mr. Perkins, then drove to my home, where I dropped it off. I worked the rest of the day with Ollie. That evening, with my father's help, I put on the brand-new tire.

My mother and father couldn't get over Mr. Perkins's generosity in purchasing the tire for me. I told them that I felt a little guilty about it. But they assured me that I should not feel that way, that he did it because I was his friend. His good friend.

I worked through Thursday, and after work Mr. Perkins gave me my paycheck. I gulped at the total. Even with the social security and insurance taken out of it, it was a lot of money.

It wasn't till the day of my next meet that I began to feel uncomfortable and worried. Suppose I came in eighth in a field of ten? I thought. Or twelfth in a field of fifteen? Or somewhere near the tail end? How would Mr. Perkins feel about it? What would he think? Would he still like me or would he be disappointed and give up on me? I don't know why I should have been more concerned about his feelings than I was about my own family's. But I was.

There were eighteen minibikes in our meet, and my number was 89. Glen Garner, riding a green mini, was 96. Was Mark paying him to force me into a spill in this meet, too? I wondered. I wouldn't be surprised; I had seen Mark there with him.

Well, I had to do the best driving I could, that's all. And keep control of my bike. That was the most important thing.

The roar was like thunder as we took off at the start of the gun. My initial fear was whether I would conquer that hill. As I stared at it in front of me it looked even steeper and more menacing than ever before. The wheels jumped and jerked. The handlebars quivered in my hands. My stomach churned. I figured I'd be lucky if my Jonny Jo and I came out of the climb with only minor battle wounds.

But we did. The mini was still roaring like a tiger as we whizzed over the top. And I was still hanging in there. Shook up, but hanging in there.

There were five laps in this heat. By the time I completed the first one, I figured I was in about eighth or ninth place. But directly ahead of me was a familiar number. 96. Glen Garner.

I gunned the engine. I didn't care where I finished in the heat, just as long as it was *ahead* of Glen Garner.

But lap one went by with Glen still ahead of me. Halfway through lap two I zipped past him on a curve. I thought he might try some funny stuff — like dodging in front of me, or yelling at me — anything to make me lose control of my bike. But he didn't.

I stayed ahead until lap three. We were near the last curve when I had a little trouble — almost capsizing after my mini struck a hump — and he sailed by me. Through the fourth lap and into the fifth he stayed ahead.

And then the heat was over, and he was still in front of me.

I felt disgusted, and hurt. He knew I had wanted to beat him, too. I could tell by his smirk.

He placed sixth, and I seventh. Nevertheless, I had done better than I expected.

❖     ❖     ❖

Our second and final heat came at one o'clock. We all had the same numbers, except that there were only fifteen entered in this heat, instead of the original eighteen. Trouble in one form or another had eliminated the other riders.

As before, it was the first climb that worried me most. But, again as before, my Jonny Jo made it. We got jarred up plenty, but we made it.

I glanced quickly around for the little green mini, and saw it at my right side. We were almost neck to neck. I gave the Jonny Jo more throttle, and pulled ahead. But by the end of the lap Garner swept past me.

"Outa my way, Baker!" he yelled at me.

He swooped in front of me, his rear wheels throwing dirt, and I thought sure I was going to ram into him. Anger blazed through me as I moved the wheel to avoid hitting him. I swear you couldn't have put a sheet of paper between his bike and mine in that fraction of a second.

He pulled ahead, and stayed ahead by about five yards going through the second and third laps.

And then, coming over a hump three-quarters of the way through lap four, my Jonny Jo flew through the air, came down with a bounce, and struck a rock that had been gouged up very recently. The front wheel swerved, almost whipping the handlebars out of my hands. But I kept it under control, managed to keep the mini from slipping into a fall, and rode on.

I inched up to Garner. I saw him glance at me for a very brief instant, then pull up in front of me. The rat, I thought. Now he was trying to keep me from passing him!

I tried to creep past him on the left side, and he moved to the left. Then I tried it to the right, and he moved to the right.

"Garner!" I yelled at him. "You're not going to stop me, no matter what you do!"

Ahead was a grade, and I turned back to his left side and powered my Jonny Jo as I had never powered her before. I sprang ahead, and by the time I reached the summit of that grade I knew that I was at least three lengths ahead of him. I could tell by the sound of his mini.

I stayed ahead of him the rest of the way, and we finished the heat, three-four.

As we rode away from the finish line Garner avoided me. He had good reason to. I saw Mark standing near the fence, his arms folded across his chest, his face twisted with disgust. I'm sure he saw me from the corner of his eye, but he never looked at me once.

I smiled to myself. Face it, Mark, I thought. Neither you, nor your pigeon, will ever scare me again.

"Good race, son!" said my father, shaking my hand. "You rode like a pro!"

"I'm proud of you, Ronnie," my mother said, giving me a hug.

But the real surprise was seeing Ollie there. He came toward me, and shook my hand.

"Beautiful ride, Ronnie!" he exclaimed. "It was just beautiful!"

I glanced past him, expecting to see someone else I knew behind him.

Ollie smiled. "Looking for Mr. Perkins? Oh, no. He would like to be here, yes. But he can't just yet. He wanted me to promise you that he will be at the next one. As a matter of fact, he is *sure* that he'll be there. And I am sure that he'll be there, too."

"Is he feeling better, Ollie?" I asked anxiously.

"A lot better," replied Ollie, his eyes shining.

I smiled, and motioned to him. "Come on. I'll introduce you to a couple of the nicest folks around. My parents."

We walked together to where my mother and father stood. But just for a moment I thought of Mr. Perkins again. He had told me how much I had filled a niche in his lonely life since he had met me. Now, suddenly I realized how much he filled a niche in mine, too.

I'll tell him that the next time I see him.

# Matt Christopher®

Muhammad Ali

Lance Armstrong

Kobe Bryant

Jennifer Capriati

Dale Earnhardt Sr.

Jeff Gordon

Ken Griffey Jr.

Mia Hamm

Tony Hawk

Ichiro

Derek Jeter

Randy Johnson

Michael Jordan

Yao Ming

Shaquille O'Neal

Jackie Robinson

Alex Rodriguez

Babe Ruth

Curt Schilling

Sammy Sosa

Tiger Woods

# Read them all!

Baseball Flyhawk

Baseball Pals

Baseball Turnaround

The Basket Counts

Body Check

Catch That Pass!

Catcher with a Glass Arm

Catching Waves

Center Court Sting

Centerfield Ballhawk

Challenge at Second Base

The Comeback Challenge

Comeback of the Home Run Kid

Cool as Ice

The Diamond Champs

Dirt Bike Racer

Dirt Bike Runaway

Dive Right In

Double Play at Short

Face-Off

Fairway Phenom

Football Fugitive

Football Nightmare

The Fox Steals Home

Goalkeeper in Charge

The Great Quarterback Switch

Halfback Attack*

The Hockey Machine

Ice Magic

Johnny Long Legs

The Kid Who Only Hit Homers

Lacrosse Face-Off

*Previously published as Crackerjack Halfback

Line Drive to Short**

Long-Arm Quarterback

Long Shot for Paul

Look Who's Playing First Base

Miracle at the Plate

Mountain Bike Mania

Nothin' But Net

Penalty Shot

The Reluctant Pitcher

Return of the Home Run Kid

Run For It

Shoot for the Hoop

Shortstop from Tokyo

Skateboard Renegade

Skateboard Tough

Slam Dunk

Snowboard Champ

Snowboard Maverick

Snowboard Showdown

Soccer Duel

Soccer Halfback

Soccer Scoop

Stealing Home

The Submarine Pitch

The Team That Couldn't Lose

Tennis Ace

Tight End

Top Wing

Touchdown for Tommy

Tough to Tackle

Wingman on Ice

The Year Mom Won the Pennant

All available in paperback from Little, Brown and Company

**Previously published as Pressure Play